Sara and the Mystery of the Thoroughbread

Anna Sellberg

Sara and the Mystery
of the Thoroughbred

I met Michael for the first time in the middle of June, I even remember it was on a Tuesday. I was riding Fandango, my gray pony, through the woods after finishing a ride over the obstacle course. I wasn't really allowed there alone because my father and mother thought it was too dangerous for me, but I'd done it often enough. Fandango chose his way confidently, and I could practically ride the course and take all the jumps blindfolded.

It was all right if it was a little dangerous – that's just what made it so exciting! Sometimes I was a little over-confident, or maybe just foolish, but usually it went just fine.

After we'd slowed to a trot and I'd loosened the reins a little bit, something made a cracking noise in the woods right near us. Fandango stiffened and halted, stuck his head in the air and pricked up his ears.

"What's up, big boy?" I asked, stroking his neck to calm him down. "It's probably only a moose. It's usually so quiet here."

There were a lot of moose in the forest around here. There weren't many things in the world that my dear sweet pony was afraid of, but moose were one of them. Another was the vet. He hated those visits. Every spring when Fandango had to have his shots, the poor thing almost fainted, even though he couldn't have felt anything but the tiniest sting from the needles.

The vet would always joke about it too. He called Fandango a scaredy-cat, and I had to admit he was right. But most of the time he was the bravest, most cool-headed pony in the world.

But it wasn't a moose that emerged from the trees. It was a slender, cinnamon thoroughbred stallion, with a saddle and bridle, but no rider! I was sure that this horse belonged to our neighbors Hans and Maggie. They lived on the farm next door, where they bred racehorses, so I wasn't just jumping to conclusions.

The stallion pricked up his ears when he saw Fandango and gave a little whinny. I jumped out of the saddle, tied Fandango to a tree and got ready to get a hold of the stallion's bridle. He was warily keeping his distance, but I didn't want him to come any closer either, since Fandango might turn away from the strange horse and kick him with his hind legs.

Just at that moment the stallion's rider appeared a little farther up the path. He seemed to have crawled out from under a bush and looked a little dazed. He had short blond hair and blue eyes, and was holding a cap in his hand. He was wearing riding pants, dirty boots and a T-shirt that must have been white when he'd put it on this morning. Everything indicated that he'd been riding fast and thrown from the saddle.

I knew right away who he must be, even though I'd

never seen him before. Our neighbor Maggie had told my mother that she'd recently hired a new stable boy. (Maggie and my mother both were nurses in the same nursing home.)

I took the stallion by the reins and led him towards the boy, who looked bewildered, I think because I was grinning as I handed him the reins. But haven't we all been thrown from our horse at an embarrassing moment? These things happen, so it didn't make sense to make any fuss about it.

"Thanks," he mumbled. "Fireflight must have been frightened by something. It seemed like there was some big animal or something in the forest."

"There are lots of moose around here," I explained. "You're the guy who took the job with Hans and Maggie, aren't you?"

He nodded and took the reins as he tried to mount the horse, but the straps on his stirrups were much too short. The stallion started to turn nervous little circles while the boy tried in vain to get one foot in the stirrup. He kept on trying, but couldn't make it, and eventually I just couldn't watch any more.

"Shall I help you? I'll hold onto him," I said as kindly as I could.

"Sure. Please…" he mumbled and his fact went all red. "If you could."

"OK," I said and took the reins from him. I scratched the stallion's forehead to distract him a little. And sure enough, he stood still for a few seconds, just long enough for the boy to get his foot in the stirrup and raise himself up into the saddle.

7

"Thanks a lot," he said and tightened the reins. "That was really nice of you. Now I can get home! That was my first time riding through the woods. There sure are a lot of paths to choose here."

"We can ride back together if you like," I suggested, and now it was my turn to tighten the reins on Fandango. "My name's Sara and this is Fandango. My dad owns the farm and pasture next to your place."

"Aha! My name's Michael, but everybody calls me Mike," he answered. "I started working for Hans and Maggie two weeks ago."

The stallion clearly wanted to get going and was dancing around as I mounted Fandango and rode towards them. Then we rode side by side over the trail. It wasn't far to Hans and Maggie's place. We left the forest – from here it was over open pastureland to their house, which was a little farther on, by the edge of the woods.

"I'll stop here," I announced, making Fandango walk in place. "I'll take another way home."

Michael looked at me a little strangely, and I knew it was a strange thing to do, since it wasn't far at all from Hans and Maggie's place to ours. It couldn't have been more than a quarter mile on the dirt road, but I preferred not to ride through Hans and Maggie's property. What Mike couldn't have known is that Hans and my dad hadn't been on good terms for years.

Actually, the whole thing was totally ridiculous. The issue was over a few square yards of forest, which they argued about endlessly and unnecessarily. My father swore up and down that it was his land, and Hans was equally insistent that it was his. The most recent step was getting a man from the government Geological Survey office to come out and re-measure everything. He took all sorts of notes and then used a topographic map to plot just what belonged to whom. It turned out that about half belonged to my father and about half belonged to Hans, so nobody knew why they'd ever begun to fight over it, and why they were still acting like enemies nobody could say.

You might think that this little episode was behind them now, but my father was as stubborn as a mule and, if he was in a bad mood he could burst out in a rage if anyone brought up the dispute. I would have bet the same thing happened at Hans' house. Even though my mother and Maggie worked together and were good friends, our families didn't socialize with each other any more.

That was also the reason why I wouldn't ride over theirproperty, even though the dirt road was the shortest route home for us.

At least for Michael it was only a very short way home. He smiled at me, and I had to smile back.

"Ok," he said, turning to go. "Thanks a lot for your help. Maybe we'll see each other again."

"I'm sure we will," I replied as I turned Fandango around and rode back towards the woods. When I'd arrived at the edge of the woods I turned around to look at the pair of them. Michael and his horse had just arrived at the farm. The rays of the setting sun lent a golden sheen to the stallion's coat. He was a beautiful sight as he stepped out with his long legs, the reins loose. I had to smile and thought to myself that this was one of the most beautiful horses I'd ever seen. And incidentally, I had to admit Michael wasn't bad either.

I put Fandango into a trot, and we rode over a narrow path along the edge of the woods. I was beginning to get hungry, and I knew it was time for dinner.

"Can you help Sophia with some jumping practice after dinner?" my father asked, once all of us were seated at the kitchen table.

All of us meant my father and mother, me and my sister Sophia. I should really count our Labrador retriever Swift too, because he always sat with us if there was any eating going on, and anxiously followed every bite we took with his big brown eyes. You never knew, sometimes a bit would come his way, and he would polish it off happily.

My sister Sophia was almost two years younger than I was, just 14. But even though we were sisters, we were completely different. We even looked totally different – I was short and stocky and had chubby cheeks, gray-green eyes and a turned-up nose. My light-blond hair was cut short, and I wanted nothing to do with makeup, since I was convinced that it wouldn't change anything with my face.

By contrast, Sophia looked like a fashion model with all that long blond hair. She had long slender legs and looked so stunning all the time that almost all the boys groveled at her feet.

I often envied her for it, but on the other hand, I hardly ever met a boy I thought would be worth the trouble.

Sophia, unlike me, was continuously in love, whether with a boy in her class, her friend Alexandra's brother, or some pop singer.

On top of that, our characters were completely different. I adored puttering around in the stable and taking care of the horses, and I enjoyed riding, even if it was rainy or cold outside.

Sophia was laziness personified. Her favorite thing to do was to lie on her bed and read one magazine after the other, and if the weather was bad she might not make an appearance in the stable all day. She had inherited my old competition pony Camigo, but she trained with him too seldom to keep him in shape for tournaments.

That was her fault alone, because Camigo was a dedicated pony who made very accurate jumps and would adapt completely to anybody riding him.

And then there was our frequent fighting. Now that I think about it, I couldn't tell you what kinds of differences of opinion we actually had, but now and then Sophia drove me nuts, and she said the same about me.

But that was absolutely not true! It only happened when she did something pretty stupid again and again. Then I couldn't help myself and had to tell her. After all, if I didn't tell her, who would?

Anyway, when Dad asked me if I'd help Sophia with her jumping that evening, I put on a sour expression. That was the last thing on earth I wanted to do!

"But she never does what I say," I shot back. Dad fixed his gaze on me as his eyebrows went up.

"She's competing next week, and she's got to practice. I have to go help my brother with his tractor."

"But I don't want to practice tonight," whined Sophia, playing with her food. "I was going to ride my bike over to Alexandra's tonight. We wanted to watch a video."

"What, you want to sit inside on such a beautiful summer evening?" cried my mother incredulously. "What a shame!"

"Hmm," grunted Sophia and shrugged her shoulders.

"First you're going to practice. And if you don't, I'll tell them you're not competing next week," my father said sternly.

Sophia sighed. "OK, OK…"

"And you're going to help her," continued Dad, looking at me.

"You only have to set up a few jumps and make sure she doesn't fall off and break all her bones."

I stared at Sophia, who stared back at me every bit as sullenly. Neither one of us was very enthusiastic about this arrangement, but we knew from Dad's voice that there was no use protesting.

My father didn't use this tone of voice with us very often, but when it was about horses, you just couldn't argue with him. Maybe it was because he'd competed himself, so he knew how much practice you needed to get any kind of results.

A little later I sat alongside our riding ring on an old chair, watching Sophia slowly warming up Camigo. She hadn't even taken the trouble to change clothes and was riding in a pink T-shirt and flowered shorts, with riding boots and a cap. It didn't exactly look professional.

Camigo didn't look like a pony who had professional experience either, even though he did. He moved over the track like he was half asleep. It looked like he'd rather go back to the pasture and continue napping.

Camigo was a good 13 hands high and gray like

Fandango. His coat had gotten lighter every year, and by now he was almost completely white.

Except for one spot, I saw when Sophia changed rein. Camigo had a big greenish-brown grass stain on the underside of his belly. My first thought was that Sophia must not have brushed him before saddling him up.

"What an attractive mark he has on his belly," I sneered at Sophia. But she just stuck up her nose as she trotted past me.

"You know how hard it is to keep him clean," she snarled and rode around me and the chair, putting a lot of space between us. "He's such a slob!"

It was clear to me that Sophia had a guilty conscience about this spot. If our dad had seen her and Camigo looking like this, he certainly would have sent her back to the stable to give Camigo a good brushing without letting them ride another step.

I laughed to myself and decided to give my sister a couple of pieces of good advice.

"Lean forward more," I called out encouragingly. "You've got to ride faster!"

"Stop screaming at me like that!" she snapped back. "He's doing just fine like this."

"He looks like a camel in the desert about to die of thirst," I replied, and a couple of seconds later Sophia stopped Camigo right in front of me.

Her face had gone all purple, partly from all her exertion and partly from anger.

"Dad said you had to set up jumps for me, not play riding teacher!" she said angrily. "I'll ride the way I want to ride, so mind your own business."

"The way you're going, you won't even get over one hurdle," I answered her. "I know Camigo. You have to give him more leg."

Sophia made a mocking grimace, put Camigo in a trot again, and once at the track, went into a canter.

"So are you gonna build the hurdles or not?" she yelled in my direction after finishing two laps. "I want to start with an oxer, a high jump, and cavaletti. Just to warm up a little."

"So why didn't you bring any of them over here yourself?" I grumbled as I got up.

We have a rule at home that whoever wants to do any jumping has to bring the obstacles to the ring. But, as usual, Sophia couldn't care less. She was just a lazy pig.

I set up the jumps she wanted and went back to my chair. Camigo was a kind of lazy too, I thought. He knew exactly when he could get out of a strenuous training session and when he couldn't. And, unfortunately, it worked every time Sophia rode him.

It just wasn't in the cards this evening. He wouldn't jump, not even over the cavaletti only a foot off the ground.

"That's because you're not riding well enough," I said maliciously. Sophia turned my way, looking like she wanted to use the whip on me.

"Shut up."

She rode towards the jump, but now she was more urgent with Camigo, and this time he jumped. But his back legs weren't high enough, and he knocked everything all over the ground.

"Next time you can set up the jumps yourself," I yelled to her while I set up the high jump again.

"Forget it!" she replied with a smirk. "Dad said you had to help me."

What could I do? There was nothing fun about helping Sophia, no matter what you tried. The sad thing was that Sophia really could ride well when she wanted to. But she never wanted to, so she didn't.

An hour later I was relaxing on the porch with a glass of cold lemonade and a horse magazine. I was reading the ads with horses for sale, because dad had once hinted he'd like to buy me a bigger horse someday. We had three horses now: Fandango, Camigo, and Maverick.

Maverick was a cinnamon Swedish crossbreed with whom Dad had once competed in tournaments all over the world. Now, however, he was retired and could usually be found out in the pasture eating to his heart's content. Nevertheless, he just loved being ridden. He could still jump like the best of them, and if you didn't know he was 32, you wouldn't have guessed he was any older than 10 or 11.

The telephone rang, and since no one else was around, I picked it up. For a moment I didn't know who was on the other end, but in a flash I realized who it was.

"Hello! Is Sara there?"

"Speaking," I answered. "Who's this?"

"It's Michael, I mean, Mike. You know, I work for your neighbors. We met today in the woods."

I felt a shiver through my entire body. Why was he calling me?

15

"You remember that horse I was riding?" he asked. His voice sounded strange.

"Of course I do," I answered him and asked curiously, "What's the matter with him?"

"He's disappeared!"

"I'm taking Swift for a walk," I said to Mom, and put on the Lab's collar.

"That's nice, dear, go ahead," she answered absently. She was lying in the hammock reading a thick book about roses. Her garden was more important to her than anything. I couldn't understand why some people loved working in the garden so much. Thank God I had my horses!

Dad was still over at his brother's place and Sophia had already left on her bike for Alexandra's house.

They lived a couple of miles from us in a small and exclusive neighborhood near Main Street. Sophia was almost always there. I assumed it was because of Alexandra's extremely good-looking brother, whom I knew she was infatuated with.

I headed for the woods while Swift took an interest in anything that came his ways, and lifted up his leg for almost every blade of grass. Although it would have been shorter to take the dirt road, Mom wasn't supposed to know I was going to Hans and Maggie's, so I was on the path along the edge of the woods.

Actually, I wasn't totally happy about going to our neighbors' place. But Mike had sounded so desperate on

17

the phone when he practically begged me to come over. I had to help him. Besides, I'd remembered that Hans and Maggie weren't home anyway. They were on a trip to England, because Maggie's sister was getting married to an Englishman.

And Mike, who didn't know a soul around here, was all alone with their five mares, their foals and 10 yearlings. All the horses were out in the pasture of course, except for Fireflight, who had only arrived a couple of days earlier.

While strolling along the edge of the woods I thought about what Mike had just said to me on the phone.

He'd come home with Fireflight a couple of hours ago and had brought him right away to the paddock next to the farmhouse. When he went outside a little later to bring him to the stable, the stallion had disappeared.

What I'd been wondering about for a while was what Hans and Maggie were planning to do with Fireflight. Hans didn't actually want any horse that needed to be trained; that much I remembered. That kind of training, in his opinion, was much too expensive, so he always sold the younger horses as soon as they'd had any success in a contest.

But Fireflight was in fantastic shape. He had exceptional muscles and had the build of a greyhound. He had all the signs of a winner.

What's more, it was unlikely that Fireflight had been bred from Hans's own stable. A few years ago, he did get two cinnamon foals, but they both had wide white blazes on their foreheads, if I remembered right.

One thing was for sure: Fireflight was like a graceful

and exotic bird among Hans and Maggie's plump mares and the sinewy, short-legged yearlings that hadn't even been broken in yet.

Mike was waiting for us at the stable. Swift loved meeting new people so he was wagging his tail like crazy. But Mike just petted him a little absent-mindedly, and we walked to the paddock together.

It was small but beautiful, and surrounded by a high white wooden fence, the back of which disappeared into a small forest.

In my eyes this was a perfect paddock, with plenty of grass for the horses and a few trees for shade when the sun was high. If I brought Fandango to such a lush pasture he'd eat himself sick, he was such a greedy thing.

"I just don't see how Fireflight could have escaped from here," said Mike, letting his eyes wander over the paddock. "The fence is at least a yard and a half high, and the last time I went to look at Fireflight he was standing right there by the trees looking happy. And nobody could have led him through the gate, because I would've seen them. I was in the stable doing a few chores, and I had a view of the front of the farmhouse the whole time."

I had to say that Mike was right. It would have been nearly impossible.

"Have you called the police?" I asked Mike, who answered with a shake of his head.

"No, I wanted to look for him myself first. I think it's kind of embarrassing. You know, I'd promised not to let this horse out of my sight for a second. That's why I was even sleeping on the sofa in the stable office."

I stared at him in disbelief.

"You sleep where? Why?"

"Come on," said Mike. "I'll tell you while we look around for him. Maybe you'll spot something I've missed."

We opened the gate into the paddock and started walking alongside the fence.

"Fireflight arrived on Monday, three days ago. The guy who brought him here was driving the most beat-up car I've ever seen, and his horse trailer looked like it came from the junkyard. He said his name was Kalle Lind and said that Fireflight belonged to him."

I nodded and Mike continued:

"I was totally surprised, because Hans hadn't said a word about any new horses coming while he was away. But the guy insisted that Fireflight was being kept here."

I nodded again, to make it clear to Mike that I understood.

"I got a stall ready and the guy gave me some oats and hay for him. I also promised him that Fireflight would get enough exercise every day. He was glad to hear it. He also said it would do him good to be in the paddock for a little while every day."

"Ok, and then what happened?" I asked breathlessly.

"When the guy had gone, I called Hans in England. It was clear that Hans knew him, he said he was a trainer at the racetrack. Hans had bred a few horses that Kalle Lind ended up breaking in."

I nodded. Of course Hans would know a lot of people in the horse-racing world.

Mike took a deep breath and went on:

"Hans told me that he had promised to Kalle to let the horse stay at the farm for a few days, but he'd thought it wouldn't be until next week. Hans said he would call the guy up to talk about things, but for the time being I was supposed to care for the horse and follow the guy's instructions."

Mike heaved a deep sigh.

"On Tuesday night, the guy called up. He sounded really nervous, and I had a lot of trouble understanding him – he was speaking real softly and there was a lot of noise in the background. It sounded like he was calling from a restaurant or something. He told me that I shouldn't let Fireflight out of my sight under any circumstances and that it was extremely important."

"When I asked him why, he said, 'Nothing must happen to my horse. There are people after my Fireflight because he's so valuable. You're completely responsible for him now, you got that?' Then he hung up."

This was getting strange, I thought as Mike went on.

"I first thought it wasn't such a big deal. It sounded like he was exaggerating everything. I mean, why wouldn't he call the police instead of asking me to look out for his horse? But last night I thought I'd better do what he said. So that was why I started sleeping in the stable office. But even so, the darn thing got away!"

Mike looked desperate, and I felt totally sorry for him. Who could have stolen Fireflight?

I looked around me. The only place where a horse could have hidden in this paddock was in among the trees and shrubs in back, but Mike was already there looking for Fireflight.

We walked farther along the fence and suddenly I noticed that all the way at the back, there were a couple of fence boards that looked a little different.

"Isn't that an old gate back there?" I asked and started towards the spot.

Mike nodded.

"Yeah, that's right, but no one uses it any more, and it's also boarded up really well. Or at least it was when I walked around the fence to check it on Tuesday before I put Fireflight in for the first time."

"Look!" I cried. "The board is gone! You can open the gate easily now." I gave the gate a gentle push with my fingertips, and it opened with a little creak. "Someone's taken the board away – this could be how Fireflight got out."

Mike's face went all white.

"Do you think someone stole him?" he asked. "Oh, I had no idea that you could open that gate…"

"I don't know what to think," I answered pensively. "How about you?"

"I don't know either," he answered slowly. "I actually was wondering if he'd just maybe jumped the fence and was on his way to a mare in heat. Stallions do that sometimes. But actually taking a nail out – no, you're right. Someone must have taken him."

I walked out through the open gate and spotted something lying on the ground. The long, thick board that until recently had kept the gate securely shut was lying in the grass a little ways away. The large, sharp nails were still sticking out from the ends of the board. I figured that whoever had removed the board would had to have tools with him. Otherwise, he'd never have gotten it loose.

There were no footprints or tracks, except for one place where a puddle of water had formed. In the dark soil there was an unusual hoofprint.

"Look there," I said, pointing to the spot. "Do you recognize that print?"

"That's Fireflight," Mike answered excitedly. "There's something a little wrong with his front hooves, so he has special horseshoes."

We looked around us, not knowing what to do next. There wasn't a horse to be seen for miles and the woods around us looked dark and impenetrable. The only sound was a blackbird pouring out his song from one of the nearby trees.

I looked around on the ground, but there were no more hoofprints anywhere to help us figure out which way Fireflight had gone.

"Should we go look for him?" asked Mike. "Maybe he's still around. If you go right, I'll go left and…"

I shook my head.

"That's not a good idea. The forest goes for miles in every direction from here. He could be anywhere. And if someone has kidnapped him, who knows how far away he could be."

Mike had to admit I was right, and we walked back through the paddock to the house in silence.

"Then I'll just have to call Hans and the police," said Mike with resignation in his voice, once we'd reached the gate to the property. "The police ought to be able to find out what direction he went off in. Maybe they could even use a bloodhound. But I just don't know what to say to Hans! I mean…"

Just then Mike was interrupted by a piercing neigh. We stared at each other in amazement. Was it Fireflight?

Suddenly something crackled in the patch of woods at the back of the paddock and then in the next moment we saw Fireflight coming our way at a gallop. He was back!

He raced right at us with his head high and a glassy stare in his eyes. I was only just able to throw myself to the side before he jumped over me, as he thundered towards the stable.

At last he started to slow down. Eventually he stood still, but with heaving flanks and raised head, with his eyes wide open from fear. He gave a panicked neigh that sounded like a trumpet call.

Mike looked like he couldn't believe his eyes. I'm sure I must have looked about the same.

"So, you're back," I remarked, thinking this wasn't the most brilliant thing I could have said, but I was at a loss for words.

"Where the heck did he come from? Could we have missed him when we were out looking for him? Maybe we didn't notice him hiding in the paddock?" Mike asked, pretty confused.

"No way," I replied. "We looked everywhere. And remember we saw that hoofprint outside the gate. No, he was gone all right. Hey look," I tried to lighten the mood a little, "now he's back."

"That wasn't exactly funny – hey, it wasn't funny at all – but I'm so happy to see him again," Mike burst out, and strode back towards the paddock.

He walked towards Fireflight, as he made calming noises to the other horses, who were looking a little shocked. Fireflight neighed once more and whipped his handsome head back and forth, all the while following Mike warily with his eyes. He took a few steps backward, as if he was planning to escape through that gate again. But Mike was able to get him under control once he'd gotten a hold of his halter.

The two of us brought Fireflight to the stable, and Mike brought him to his stall at the back. While he went to fetch a bucket of lukewarm water and a sponge, I took a look around me. I hadn't been in Hans and Maggie's stables since he and Dad had started their dispute and that was long enough ago that I couldn't remember anything about them.

The corridor between the stalls was wide and the stalls themselves were roomy and light. Everything had been freshly painted in green and white and it all looked so nice I felt a little pang of jealousy. It looked very different from our own shabby stable, which was in reality nothing but a converted old henhouse.

I'd been complaining to my father for a few years that we needed to repaint the stable, but he claimed the paint was too expensive. He was planning to build new stalls in the cowshed once he'd sold the last calves. I only wondered when he was planning to start. He hadn't mentioned it for a long time now, although he'd sold the last calf around a year ago. And instead of raising new ones he was working as a driver for a transportation company in town.

One day soon – the day when I got my new horse –

we'd be more or less forced into painting the stable. I knew for sure now that it would have to be just these colors. No question.

I stood outside the stall watching how Mike examined Fireflight to see if anything had happened to him. He stroked the stallion's legs and carefully felt along his spine.

"It keeps getting weirder," said Mike guardedly as he walked up to me. "He doesn't have a scratch on him anywhere, and he looks just fine, except look here…"

Mike pointed to Fireflight's rear and I went into the stall to look. Right under his tail, almost under the hocks, the skin was chafed at the same place on both back legs. You could almost make out abrasions, as if Fireflight had been rubbing against something with all his might.

"Strange. What could it be?" I asked. We stood there staring at Fireflight and pondering the situation for a while.

A little later I left the stall and Mike followed me. As he locked Fireflight's stall carefully, he looked lost in thought.

"You have to call the police now," I told him.

Mike shook his head.

"What am I supposed to tell them? Hello police, Fireflight disappeared, but, uh, I guess he's come back…"

"But he didn't disappear all by himself," I replied. "Someone broke open the gate and took him. It would have been different if Fireflight had just left on his own."

"Could it just be some kids playing a trick?" he asked

pensively. "Or a couple of horse-crazy girls who wanted a free ride…"

I shook my head.

"I don't think kids would have the tools to pull out that board. They must have been a grownup to manage something like that."

"Ok. I think you're right," admitted Mike. "Someone could have tried to steal Fireflight. But if I call the police now, they'll just say that I wasn't watching him well enough. That'll put Hans in a good mood."

I nodded. Hans was famous for his bad temper so I could understand Mike wanting to avoid one of his outbursts. I would have done the same in his place.

"Well, Fireflight is back now, and in one piece, except for those strange places on his hind legs, but they don't look too bad," Mike said, and gave the stallion a friendly slap on his neck.

"I'll just have to watch you like a hawk from now on," he continued and hung the halter up on the outside wall of the stall.

Then he went back in and washed the stallion with lukewarm water. It looked for all the world like Fireflight was relaxing with his bath, now that his little adventure was over. He wasn't moving a bit and was clearly enjoying himself thoroughly.

I looked at my watch. It was now almost 10 p.m. and it wouldn't be much longer before Mom would be wondering just when I was planning to come home.

"I've got to go home," I said, and Mike gave a nod.

"Sure, I understand," he replied. "Listen, it was great of you to come over and help me. You're the only one I know around here; that's why I called you up. I hope that was all right – I hear your dad and Hans don't exactly get along."

"No problem," I said. "I wouldn't have come if it wasn't OK."

We both had to smile, and I couldn't help but feel a warm rush when our eyes met. Mike had a very special smile that sent shivers down my spine. Bashfully I switched my gaze to Swift, who had been watching us. I wasn't at all used to a boy smiling at me like that. It was totally different. On the one hand it was a little exciting, but yet a little, well, almost creepy. It felt like I was ashamed of something, but there was nothing to be ashamed of.

To change the subject I asked, "So, are you going to sleep in the stable again tonight?"

Mike nodded.

"Yup, that's the plan," he said emerging from the stall. "I have to. I promised that guy I would. But take it from me that I really don't feel like it. I'd much rather crawl into my own bed and fall asleep and forget the whole thing."

"If anything happens, you can always call me," I offered. "I have my own cell phone – I got it for my birthday last month from my grandparents."

That seemed to lift Mike's spirits.

"Do you mean it? Wow, great! What's your number?"

I told it to him and he wrote it down on a scrap of paper he tore from a feed sack. He mumbled it a few times under his breath. It was clear to me he wanted to know it by heart.

"But now I really have to go," I said and gave a little tug on the leash. "Come on, Swift. Time to go home."

Swift got up slowly, stretched, wagged his tail and went over to Mike, who gave him a pat on the head.

"It was incredibly nice of you to come over. I'll call you – if anything happens," he said as we walked to the stable door together. He didn't exactly look happy, and I could believe he was pretty uneasy. I would have loved to stay, but I just couldn't. Maybe he didn't think so either. Anyway, I felt rotten leaving him there like that, right after someone obviously had tried to steal Fireflight.

"You can call me any time. I'm just as curious about this whole thing as you," I continued and tried to cheer him up.

"Call me, even if it's in the middle of the night. I keep my phone next to my bed." Mike nodded and said he'd be glad to take me up on it. We said good-bye outside of the stable. He wanted to go into the house and get a bite to eat before going to sleep on the office couch.

Swift and I strode along the narrow path home. My thoughts kept milling around all the way back, but when I'd gotten home, I knew only that I didn't know a thing, especially what it was all about.

The next morning I awoke early. Usually I could sleep pretty late, but I was wide awake now. There was no point in turning over again and trying to go back to sleep either. I knew I was wide awake, even though it wasn't even 5 a.m.

I stuck my hand out from under the covers and lifted the shade. The sun was already up and a gentle breeze that made its way in through the small opening in the window gently rustled my white curtains.

After I'd had a deep yawn and a good stretch, my thoughts returned to last night, to Fireflight, and to Mike.

I hadn't met anyone like him before. Maybe that was because I'd never really sought out the company of boys. Almost all the boys in my grade at school still acted like children. Even though we'd finished 10th grade, you wouldn't know any of them were much older than twelve. They were mostly concerned with making a lot of noise and getting in fights with each other. To get one of them to put a sentence together was an impossible task.

Even for Sebastian, who I'd gone to the movies a couple of times with last spring, and who even tried to kiss me on the last day of school in back of the auditorium, which didn't work at all (very embarrassing!).

But Mike was another story. He had treated me like somebody his own age, even though he had to be 18 – I supposed. He looked it, and I knew he had a driver's license. I felt more grown up when I was around him. He also seemed to care what I thought or felt about things.

I got out of bed and looked out the window. Fandango and Camigo spent their nights in the stable to prevent them eating too much grass and getting fat. But Maverick was out grazing in the morning sun. His golden-red coat was gleaming and I couldn't suppress a smile. He looked fine, good old Maverick. I could only hope that my next horse would be as wonderful as he was. The best would be a thoroughbred. A big, long-legged gelding, that would clear every obstacle, who could run cross-country with the best, was comfortable with dressage and loved jumping.

But where could we find a horse like that? I had no idea. My father and I had been looking at the "horse for sale" advertisements for more than six months, and we'd found nothing. Either the horses were too expensive, or there was something else very wrong with them. I fantasized about my dream racehorse but in the meantime, I still had Fandango.

I suddenly got the urge to go riding. This morning was simply too beautiful to spend lying in bed. I slipped into my riding pants, pulled on a sweater, and tiptoed down the stairs so as not to wake anyone else. Even Swift was still sleeping and didn't move when I passed him, except to lift an eyelid. He watched me slip on my sneakers and fell back to sleep on his trusty old blanket.

Fandango pricked up his ears when I entered the stable, and Camigo whinnied softly. I gave both horses some hay and stroked Fandango's coat. He willingly opened his mouth for me to put in the bit, and looked very happy when he was led unsaddled outside, to the old bench against the stable wall.

I'd decided to ride bareback, but that didn't make mounting him any easier, and it took some time for me to get up on Fandango's back. He couldn't understand what I was trying to do at all, and was all over the place until at last I got him still for a few seconds and threw one leg over his back, then got myself into a comfortable position.

We rode out along the path that I usually took, towards the woods. The sun was shining and the air smelled like horse, summer, pine needles, and all the other smells that make summer so fantastic. I loosened the reins and Fandango went on with a light step. I was getting into a fine mood sitting on his back like this.

What a good idea this was, to get out of bed so early. I gave Fandango's neck a caress as I told myself to remember how this felt and that I should do it more often. Of course it would only work if I could manage to wake up on time.

In no time I was at Hans and Maggie's place. I had chosen a path along the paddock with the gate where Fireflight had been grazing the day before. I couldn't help sneaking up to the gate and looking at it from up close. It was closed and locked, and the board that had been thrown in the grass was now up against the fence.

Mike and I had completely forgotten the gate last night. We'd been so preoccupied with catching Fireflight that we hadn't thought about anything else. I could only remember that I'd opened the gate wide when we'd gone looking for him. Who had closed it? Fireflight himself couldn't have done it every easily. And who had put the board back? I knew it had been lying in the grass a little ways away.

Of course it could have been Mike. He could have made a last round before turning in and closed everything up. But I didn't know that yet.

I examined the gate carefully and tried to go over what had actually happened yesterday. Someone had captured Fireflight and taken him with them. Stolen him! That much was very clear. The paddock had been empty when Mike and I had walked along the fence, I was sure of that.

Later the thieves had brought Fireflight back to the paddock, led him through the gate and, possibly, closed the gate behind him. But wasn't that too crazy for words? Who would take the trouble to steal a horse, just to bring him back?

Suddenly I thought of something. Not far from the farm there was an old road through the forest. Nobody used it any more. Sophia and I had ridden there sometimes because you never saw cars there. The road didn't go anywhere, it just stopped at a big clearing, which had since been overgrown with shrubs and brush.

Anybody stealing a horse had to have a car and a trailer. Maybe he (or she – it could just as easily be a female horse thief, I thought) had taken the narrow road to leave the two vehicles there.

33

The supposed perpetrator could then have walked the two hundred yards from the farm to the clearing. There were several paths to take, including the old almost completely overgrown trail through the woods, which led directly to the gate that had been broken. For someone used to working with horses it would be no trouble at all to catch Fireflight, lead him to the horse trailer waiting there, and drive away with him.

But why had the thief brought Fireflight back to the paddock and shut him in again?

I couldn't come up with any explanation. I decided to ride over to the old road to get a better look. Maybe I'd see tire tracks or something else that could shed some light on the situation.

While Fandango and I rode towards the old road, I felt my stomach tighten up. A horse that disappears and then reappears in one piece is already kind of odd. The thought that, on top of that, a horse thief was lurking around in our woods didn't really put my mind at ease. To be honest, I nearly turned back a few times, but Fandango and I reached the road very soon and once we were that far I got the courage to keep going. I could, of course, have it all wrong. In fact, I was sure I was wrong – at least I tried to convince myself I was.

When we got onto the road, Fandango started to stamp and paw and dance around nervously. Of course he wanted to speed up a little now. But I kept him under control, and talked to him softly to calm him down. How could I look for clues if we were galloping along at full speed? I also didn't know if I could hold on if I gave Fandango free rein. Now and then he had made some leaps which had almost thrown me off. I knew that with no saddle, I had little chance of staying on in the long run if he were to make another leap like that.

We rode all the way to the turning point near the clearing at a slower pace, even though Fandango wanted to gallop the whole time. When we got there, we turned around and rode over the same road back to where it crossed another forest path that turned into a gravel road. This road went almost all the way to the neighborhood where Sophia's friend Alexandra lived.

There wasn't a clue anywhere, no sign of a car or horse. I guided Fandango back into the woods, over the narrow path leading back to our house. It would have been cool, of course, if I'd found some clue and could tell Mike about it. Nonetheless I was relieved that I hadn't.

We'd gone about twenty yards into the woods when I heard the hum of a motor behind us. The sound got closer and closer, and my heart started to beat louder and louder.

Who was it and what were they doing here in the middle of the woods this early in the morning?

I made Fandango stand still and peered through the trees at the road which by now was a little behind us. It was hemmed in by bushes and brush and you wouldn't see anything if you weren't looking out for it. I was able to see a light blue pickup truck with a trailer behind it, making its way over the narrow path to the clearing.

I felt hot and cold at the same time. My heart was beating a thousand times a minute and my head was spinning. What should I do? The only thing I could think of was to warn Mike as quickly as I could. What if this was the horse thief, and he was coming back!

But how could I get in touch with him? I realized that I'd left my cell phone at home. How was I supposed to sneak past the thief to Hans and Maggie's farm? Could I get there if I stuck to the woods? Maybe so, I thought, and turned Fandango around.

I pressed my thighs firmly into Fandango's flanks and he began to trot, happy to not be plodding along like an old work horse. He tore off and it was all I could do to hang onto his mane and keep my balance.

After a while the path opened onto a wider one, and from there out it was familiar territory for Fandango. I tried to slow him down, knowing what was going on in his head, but I didn't have a chance once he was at a gallop. Very quickly, the first obstacle of the course appeared in front of us.

"Stop!" I screamed, but Fandango completely ignored me.

He adored galloping and jumping over fences. If my father had been there, I'm sure he would have said that this was what I deserved for all the times I'd gone jumping without him or Sophia there.

Fandango took the first fence, a small structure of birch trunks, with no problems. Then he went for the next one, which was rather high and covered with old pine branches. I clamped myself to his mane when I saw Fandango speeding toward it. It was impossible to have any influence on him at all under these circumstances. The only thing I could think of was that it wouldn't be long before I lost my balance and fell to my death.

It was almost miraculous the way we sailed lightly over the branches and landed together on the other side. After that, the path turned to the right and then sloped gently downhill. Halfway down the slope was a new obstacle, and my face went white when I realized what we were heading for. But Fandango was an experienced competitor. He slowed his gallop, pushed off and made it smoothly over.

I realized that it really wasn't that hard riding without a saddle. We could both get over the obstacles without thinking too much about it, because we'd been over this one a hundred times before. But still I was clinging to his mane to keep my balance.

The path went downhill again, and we approached a brook. Fandango just pricked up his ears as he went over it, only stretching his legs a little more than for a normal stride. Then he collected his hind legs and pushed off to take the slight uphill at full speed. I loosened the reins, since both of my hands were clutching at his mane. Even on the uphill he'd hardly lost any speed. Once we were at the top, though, I was able to get the reins a little tighter, and I tried to get him to stop.

"Whoa! Hold still, you rascal!" I snarled and pulled on the reins with all the strength I had left.

Fandango reluctantly stopped his trot, shook his head violently back and forth, and danced from one foot to the other. He wanted to keep running, but I wouldn't budge an inch. He simply had to stay still now. To our right was Hans and Maggie's farm, and that's where we were headed.

Eventually he let me guide him, and I was able to pick

our way through the trees. There was no path, and I wanted to keep out of sight as much as possible in this last stretch. Soon the brilliant white stable was in front of us. I trotted over the road to the stable and made Fandango stop right in front of the door. I leaped from his back and knocked loudly on the door.

Inside the stable, Fireflight neighed loudly and exuberantly, and a few seconds later I heard the lock creaking. The stable door opened and there was Mike looking out at me. Evidently he'd slept in a sweater and jeans. He looked half asleep and his blond hair was sticking out in all directions. I had obviously woken him up.

"What's going on?" he mumbled with a yawn. "What are you doing here, and what time is it?"

"The horse thieves!" I panted. "Those people who tried to steal Fireflight, they've come back. I saw a car with a horse trailer turning onto the old road through the woods. At least it looked like they were going that way."

Mike scratched behind his ears. He looked like none of this had made any sense to him.

"Old road through the woods? What are you talking about?" he asked, looking as confused as ever. "Would you be so kind as to explain everything, slowly?"

I took a deep breath and tried to keep it clear.

"A little into the woods, just a couple hundred yards from here, is an old road through the woods, and…"

Breathlessly I told Mike what had happened, and what I suspected. Mike thought for a while, then disappeared into the stable to bring Fireflight his breakfast. A moment later he came outside and stood looking out pensively at the woods for a long time.

"What do we do now? Should I ride back to the road and see if they're still there?" I asked, and to my relief Mike shook his head no. He ran his hands through his hair and smiled at me.

"Well, that puts a few pieces of the puzzle together," he said finally. "It looks to me like they discovered that road by chance and thought it was a perfect place to load Fireflight in the trailer after taking him from the paddock. After all, the farm is at the end of the road. It'd be too risky driving all the way down the road with a trailer. They'd be too easily seen, especially since they'd have to ride right past the farm."

"But why would they bring Fireflight back to the paddock?" I wondered. "I mean, that's completely insane!"

Mike thought a second and snapped his fingers. "They couldn't get him in the horse trailer! Now I'm beginning to understand. Those funny scraped-up places I saw on his back legs – they must be from long straps or ropes."

Mike walked back into the stable and Fandango and I followed him.

"When that guy came to bring Fireflight here on Monday, Fireflight went nuts in the trailer," said Mike. "He thrashed around and once we'd cut him loose, he shot out like a bullet. That means he doesn't like traveling."

"Hmm. That sounds like a good explanation," I said and Mike nodded in agreement.

He entered the stall and ran his hand over Fireflight's coat, which felt soft as velvet and shone like silk. Except for that bit of fur on his hind legs, where it looked like something had broken through his thin delicate skin.

"I think there were two or three of them," Mike proposed. "They must have tried to pull him into the trailer with a rope. When that didn't work, they brought him back to the paddock, hoping nobody noticed that he'd been gone. It looks like they want to make another stab at it as soon as they can."

We smiled at each other and Mike gave another huge yawn.

"I really need a cup of coffee or I won't survive this," he said, still smiling. "You have no idea how horrible it is sleeping on that couch."

"But aren't you scared they'll come back and steal Fireflight while you're having breakfast?" I asked, and realized immediately how stupid that sounded.

"No," said Mike with a smile, "because those guys have no idea that they might get caught. I'll lock the stable, and besides, I can see the whole place from the kitchen window. If they come I'll call the police. Hey, would you like some breakfast?"

I looked at my watch and couldn't believe how late it was. On the one hand, my parents and my incredibly nosy sister would be starting to wonder where I'd gone off to. On the other hand, I really wanted to drink a cup of coffee with Mike. What should I do?

Of course I chose the second option and after I'd put Fandango in an empty stall and given him some hay, I trudged after Mike into the little room where he lived. There was an old cot for him to sleep on. I knew that this was where Hans and Maggie's stable boys lived, but I'd never been there myself. The kitchen looked quaint with its white walls, yellow cupboard doors, gingham curtains and two thriving red geraniums in pots on the windowsill.

Mike is doing all right here, I thought. It sure was a lot neater and tidier than my room.

I took a seat on the edge of a kitchen chair. I felt excited but at the same time a little nervous that I'd gone with Mike to his room alone just like that. And we hadn't known each other all that long. My heart was beating faster than usual, and I didn't really know how I should act or what I should say. So I just sat there, not saying a word, and watched Mike make coffee and take out two mugs, milk, and sugar.

"I'm afraid there's only some bread," he said and looked at me. "Is that all right?"

"Sure," I answered. "Can I help you with anything?"

"No, thanks, you just stay right where you are," he

41

said and put a plate of bread on the table. Then he opened the cupboard door and mumbled something I couldn't make out.

"I'm sorry, but it looks like I'm out of butter and bacon and eggs and everything, there's only some blueberry jam. How about that? I think it's really good on bread."

"Anything's fine," I said.

I could be looking at a piece of cardboard with ketchup on it, I thought, as long as I could be sitting in the kitchen with Mike and feel the butterflies in my stomach and a little...

Just then the telephone rang and Mike answered it.

"Hello," he said in a gentle voice and I was sure it was Hans asking how everything was.

But it wasn't Hans. Mike looked confused and shook his head a little, and with his outstretched arm pointed to a ball-point pen on the table. I grabbed it quickly and gave it to him along with a newspaper that was on the table.

"No, we're not expecting a package... Oh, yeah, that... I didn't get any message. Where can I pick it up?... OK, could you give me the number..."

Mike scribbled some numbers on the margin of the newspaper and hung up.

"Strange," he said, raising his eyebrows. "That was the post office. They've got an important package there for Hans. But Hans never said anything about me picking up anything from the post office."

He looked at the number that he'd written down and gave a little frown.

"The post office doesn't usually call you, do they?" I

asked suspiciously. "They put a notice in your mailbox if you're not home, and if you don't come for it after a while, they send you a reminder."

"Exactly," answered Mike and looked at the kitchen clock, which said 7:15 a.m. "And why would they call so early in the morning? They must have just gotten to work."

"And you know what," I said even more mistrustfully, "it's a long way from here to the nearest post office. We've never had to go pick up packages there. I know that. Our neighbors don't have to either. And anyway, the post office isn't open this early."

We stared at each other, and I knew we were both thinking the same thing: it couldn't have been the post office. But who was it?

Suddenly the telephone rang again. We were both so startled that we jumped out of our seats a little. I saw Mike hesitate for a second before picking it up.

"Hello?" he said cautiously, and I could see his whole body was tense.

Was it the same person who had just called? The relieved expression on Mike's face told me it was someone else.

"You'll come get him? Fine. No, but… I have a couple of questions I'd like to ask you, though. Why did you bring Fireflight here? And why… Hello… hallo!"

Mike talked in vain into the receiver. Slowly he hung up.

"That was Fireflight's owner," he said. "He'll come get him tomorrow or the next day."

"Good," I said. "That's great."

43

"What a relief," he said and ran his fingers through his hair. Then he looked at me and smiled.

"Boy, will I be happy when this whole thing is over with!"

"But what will you do with him until then?" I asked cautiously. "What if someone steals him in the meantime?"

"I'll keep an eye on him and keep him locked in the stable until then."

"I'd still call the police," I urged him.

Mike laughed.

"And what should I tell them? That Fireflight disappeared but came back and then someone called me and told me a lie about a package?"

"Don't forget I saw the car and trailer on the road to the clearing," I reminded him. "What were they up to there? Who's going to drive around in the woods with a horse trailer at 5:30 a.m. on a summer morning?"

Mike smiled at me and cocked his head a little. The way he was looking at me… I felt my stomach jump.

"It could just be somebody who got lost. If I remember right, there's a riding school on the other side of that ritzy neighborhood, isn't there? And we don't even know if it was the same guy who called about the package. That's why I've got to make a call now. It could be that Hans just forgot to tell me about it."

I nodded.

"Sure, but…"

"The police would just laugh at me and tell me to forget the whole thing and stop listening to ghost stories," Mike replied.

We sat for a while and sipped our coffee, which was strong and hot. I actually couldn't stand coffee, but it wasn't too bad with milk and sugar in it.

After I'd emptied my cup, I realized I really had to get going.

"Listen, I've got to go," I said. "My family is going to be wondering what's happened to me."

"OK," he answered, spreading jam on a third piece of bread. "If anything happens, I'll let you know."

"Please do," I said and got up.

"And I'll call the police anyway," added Mike. "It couldn't hurt to let them know what the situation is. Just to be on the safe side. Then I'll tell them how that guy tried to trick us."

"I'll make sure I have my cell phone with me," I said. "What's your phone number, anyway?"

I wrote down both his cell phone number and the one at the farm and put the scrap of paper in my pocket. Then Mike walked me to the stable and unlocked the door. When I'd harnessed up Fandango and led him outside, Mike gave him a swat on his back to help me off, and I set off towards the woods.

It was almost 8:30 a.m. when I got home. Sliding off Fandango's back I realized I didn't know how I was going to explain this to my parents. After a long pause, I decided to tell them I'd just been on a long ride through the woods.

And of course if nobody asked, I didn't have to say anything at all.

The whole house looked asleep. The odds were good that nobody would be interested in where I'd been all morning. I brought Camigo and Fandango to their paddock and walked to the house, where Mom was having breakfast on the porch.

"Did you have a nice ride, dear?" she asked a little absently as she flipped through the morning paper.

I mumbled a "yes" and went into the kitchen to get a glass of chocolate milk to take the coffee off my breath. My little sister was apparently still asleep and Dad must have already taken off to see his brother, since the car was gone.

I thought with relief that it sure had been a nice ride, and had to yawn.

A couple of hours ago I had been wide awake, but now I was incredibly tired. I dragged myself upstairs and crawled into bed under my soft blue wool blanket. Wow, was I beat! I closed my eyes and felt sleep taking over slowly. Outside my window a bumblebee was droning monotonously, and my last thought was how wonderful it was summer vacation, and we could sleep whenever we felt like it.

But I was wrong. Suddenly the door burst open and in came my dear little sister, in her bathrobe, with a towel over her hair and with some green glop on her face that looked like mashed avocado.

She looked an awful lot like a space alien wrapped in pink terrycloth. The green stuff on her face was probably the latest acne remedy. At the moment I wished she were in outer space, especially as I became aware of the curious leer in her eyes through the green. The beast sat down at the foot of my bed, while I demonstratively pulled the blanket over my head and held my eyes shut.

"And where were you all morning?" she asked at last, and I glared at her between my eyelids.

"Out. I went for an early ride," I answered. "Nothing you'd be interested in. Now go away, I'm tired."

"Aha… So what were you doing at Hans and Maggie's? You can tell me that much at least."

Her nosy question startled me, and I sat up in bed with annoyance.

"None of your business," I snarled at her. "And how do you know I was there anyway?"

My sister laughed a little and filed at her nails with an emery board.

"Right. Well, now, I was up early too, and when I looked out my window – you know I can see all the way to their farm – I could just make out how a cute blond guy was helping you onto your horse. I must admit I was somewhat surprised."

I didn't know what to say. This was really bad. My sister never, and I mean never ever, got up before 10:30 a.m. if she didn't have to. Why, out of all the mornings in the world, did she have to wake up so early today?

I decided to be open with her. What else could I do?

"OK," I mumbled. "I just wanted to stop by and see that guy. He's really nice."

"Oh yeah, Mike," she said, trying to sound casual. "You're right, he's cute. I've seen him before. It was Friday night, at the Starlight."

"The Starlight," I repeated in surprise and stared at my sister. "What were you doing there? You can't get in there unless you're 18!"

The Starlight is really a place for grownups, and not a teenage disco where Sophia would hang out.

"Come on, we were only outside," she said haughtily, studiously examining her fingernails as she kept on filing. "Alexandra and I passed it on the way to the bus stop after we went to the movies."

"Don't lie, the bus stop's not in that direction," I said. "And what was he doing there?"

"Nothing, he just was on his way in," answered Sophia, laughing at me. "Then we went home. Even though we could have gotten in if we wanted to, you know. Alexandra's brother knows one of the bouncers there."

"But how did you know it was Mike that you saw there?" I interrupted her. I knew she was totally nuts about Alexandra's big brother, and I didn't need to hear her go on again about how incredible he was.

"Alexandra knew," said Sophia and shrugged her shoulders. "Her parents get along with Hans and Maggie, unlike some parents I know. Did you know that Mom and Dad are going out tonight?"

"No," I said. "Where?"

"To George and Mia's. I don't think I'll go. How about you?"

George is my father's brother, and Mia is his wife. Being invited to a barbecue at their house was absolutely the most boring thing in the world I could imagine. There were always a lot of grownups, and they talked about boring stuff all the time, and expected that the "young folks" would entertain ourselves even though there was nothing to do there. No way was I going!

"I'm staying here," I said. "No," teased my sister, "I know, you're going back to see Mike."

I made a face at her. "That's none of your business. And promise me you won't say a word to Mom and Dad. Promise!"

I glared at her menacingly and hoped that she was convinced that I meant it.

"OK," she said with a nod, "but you have to promise me not to tell them something."

"What?"

"Alexandra and I are going into town tonight – at least that's the plan. Her brother and one of his friends asked if we wanted to see a movie and then go out somewhere afterwards."

I sat there not moving for a while. On the one hand, I didn't feel good about my little sister going into town all by herself without Mom and Dad knowing about it. On the other hand, she wouldn't be in my way if Mike needed my help.

For the second time today I seriously didn't know what to do. But finally I nodded slowly in consent.

"OK, I won't say anything. But make sure you get the last bus back, and only go with Alexandra and nobody else, OK? Promise me?"

Sophia grinned her cunning grin.

"You and your deadlines," she said. "That bus was your idea, and I'll come home when I'm ready. But that's fine, you've got a deal!"

From her voice I could tell that I could count on her. My sister can be really nice when she wants to.

I awoke and looked at my alarm clock with bleary eyes. It was already 11:30 a.m. and that meant that I'd be expected downstairs soon. Usually lunch was our big meal when the family was all at home.

I was somehow not feeling very good. I'd had one of those weird dreams that you get when you sleep in the daytime.

Fandango was in it, and the two of us were in a dark forest. Everything looked dangerous and threatening, but I knew all my questions would be answered if we found what I was looking for. But I couldn't find it, and woke up.

I heard the door open and my mother looked in.

"Hey, are you still sleeping?" she asked, surprised. "Lunch is almost ready."

"I'll be right down," I said and got up.

We ate out on the porch. Mom had made fish and boiled potatoes, and for my sister, who didn't like fish, meatballs.

Just then my father drove up with the trailer on the car. He seemed in a very good mood, and when he sat down with us, I knew why.

"I just got a whole lot of birch logs from George," he said enthusiastically, "so I can build new jumps. You two want to help me?"

"Not me," said Sophia quickly. "I don't really feel like it – I wanted to go swimming with Alexandra and a couple of friends."

"And you?" Dad turned to me with that penetrating stare he had when he wanted one of us to help him with something he was planning.

I nodded hesitantly. I didn't really feel like going to the woods to work on a hot summer afternoon. On the other hand, a couple of new jumps would be just fine and I didn't have any other plans either.

After lunch Sophia rode her bike to her friend's, while Dad and I took the car and trailer and drove into the woods. Dad knew exactly where he wanted to put the jumps, so we could get going right away.

The birch logs weren't really thick, but very heavy and it took a lot of work to put up a relatively wide oxer. As soon as we were finished with it I took a look and felt a jab in the pit of my stomach. This was a really long one, and I knew it wouldn't be so easy for Fandango to get over it.

With a little work and patience, though, he'd make it. Fandango was hard-working and brave, and he loved jumping. However, he wasn't a real competition horse, and that's why I had a guilty conscience. I should really have trained more with him but it was unimaginably boring riding around in endless circles. So my thoughts stopped there.

When our work was done, we got back in the car and

51

drove home. Now I had a burning desire to go to the swimming hole. Not far from the house was a small lake. It was mostly overgrown with cattails and other weeds, but there was one place with a tiny beach, and the sand was fine and clean under your feet for a few yards into the water, where it suddenly dropped off. Aside from my own family, there were almost never any other people there.

As soon as we came home, I changed into my suit and took off on my bike for the swimming hole. Even from far away I could hear voices and laughter and, to my surprise, the little beach had already been taken over by my sister, Alexandra, her brother, and a few other people I only knew by sight. They looked like they were having fun. I stood there, unable to make up my mind, and thought for a while.

I had no desire at all to have anybody around me, and certainly not my sister's noisy friends. So I slowly rode home. Instead of a nice dip I had a long cool shower, then went out to the hammock and tried to think, which in the afternoon heat was easier said than done. So I spent the time just lying there, dozing away now and then, and thinking more or less about nothing.

Suddenly, my cell phone started ringing and at the first ring I sat bolt upright, even though I'd set the volume as low as possible. My heart started to pound and I was completely awake now, because I thought it could only be Mike. To my great disappointment it was my little sister.

"I'm at Alexandra's," she said cheerily, "and they invited me to stay to dinner. Can you tell Mom and Dad?"

"Why don't you just call them yourself?" I asked. I heard a lot of noise in the background at Alexandra's house.

"Nobody answered," Sophia explained, but I knew she wasn't telling the truth. We had a huge ringer installed on the outside of the house so if the phone rang you could hear it from anywhere on the property. I certainly would have been able to hear it just now.

"Oh, come on," I said to her. "You're lying!"

My sister gave a deep sigh.

"I don't want to talk to Mom. I know you can stay home if you want tonight, but she's going to insist I come with them to that barbecue and I don't want to!"

That was so typical of my sister, I had to snicker. Now I would be the one to defiantly tell Mom and Dad that wild horses couldn't drag me to see my uncle and his family. More than that, Sophia knew that if she talked to Mom, Mom would drive over to Alexandra's right away and take her home.

"OK," I said at last. "I'll tell Mom and Dad hi from you and that you're at Alexandra's. But promise me you'll get home on time tonight. If you don't, I'll kill you!"

"Yeah, yeah," she sighed. "Do you know, sometimes you sound just like Mom? It's not like you. But don't worry, I'll get home on time. Bye-bye!"

I hung up, climbed out of the hammock and went to find my mother, who was probably kneeling in front of one of her flower beds, praying to the roses. I found her in the kitchen, though, washing her hands.

She said hi when she saw me, and asked, "Hey, want

53

to drive into town with me? I need to get a better shovel and some more weedkiller."

I nodded. Of course I could go with her into town, even though it was as hot as a sauna out there. It would be more fun than lying around in my hammock not knowing what to do.

I told her about Sophia's phone call, and she sighed and shook her head.

"I just don't know what's got into her," she said. "Sophia's changed a lot recently. And she was always such a sweet little girl."

"I'm sure it's puberty," I informed her.

My mother looked at me thoughtfully.

"Do you think? Well, I guess that could be all it is, at least I think so. Well, she'll get over it. I just hope she doesn't do anything crazy in the meantime. It's good she's still friends with Alexandra. She's bright and sensible."

I thought, but said nothing, that Mom had no idea at all that Alexandra was the wilder of the two, and my threat to Sophia was serious: if Sophia didn't come home on time tonight, I would really ... well, I'd do something awful, that was clear.

A little later my mom and I were in the car headed into town. I'd rolled the window on my side all the way down, there was good music on the radio, and the warm breeze coming in smelled of summer. I closed my eyes and enjoyed the ride.

It was all perfect, until the moment Mom had had enough of the music. She searched until she found a talk show on the subject of old folks' homes. Of course this was something important to her, because she and Maggie had to deal with old people in their line of work all the time. I made a grimace, but she didn't seem to notice me, already engrossed. This was really her kind of show!

In town we went our separate ways. My mother wanted to go to the hardware store on Main Street, and I sauntered over to the tack shop around the corner. I hardly had any money with me, but it was still fun to look at all the great things you could buy – if you just had a little more money.

It was stuffy and hot in the store. I stood looking at the horse books. There was a thick book on the shelf about military riding that I wanted very much, and I looked through it carefully. It was full of gorgeous color photos and it was beautiful to see how the riders could fly over so many different kinds of jumps.

I was so lost in thought that I didn't notice the buzzer at the door announcing that someone else had come in. I only looked up from the book when a man's voice asked about an inexpensive halter. A big strong-looking man was at the counter in a checked shirt and worn jeans. Bert, the owner of the store, pointed the section out to him.

"How big does it have to be?" he asked the customer.

I kept quiet as a mouse and listened hard.

"It's for a big horse," answered the man. "But really, I just need the cheapest thing you've got, nothing fancy."

"Here's a decent one, it's only…" started Bert, but the man didn't even let him finish his sentence.

"I'll take it."

I heard the rustling noise it made as Bert packed up the halter and a few moments later the man had paid and left the store.

I put the book back on the shelf and walked around, gazing at the other equipment. Bert was behind the counter putting price tags on new halters.

"Hey there, how's it going with the contests?" he asked me, because he knew I'd been competing with Fandango.

"Really well, thanks," I replied and smiled at him. "Oh, what nice halters."

Bert nodded and held up a halter with beautiful designs in dark blue, green and red.

"This one would look good on your horse," he said with a grin. "It's not incredibly expensive either, just twenty bucks. And it comes with a matching lead."

I took the halter in my hand. It felt soft and yet very sturdy and strong. I would have bought it right away, but as usual there was the slight problem of finances.

"I can't really afford this right now," I mumbled shyly, "but I do need a bag of rubber bands and a roll of white tape for his mane."

Bert put them in a paper bag for me, and after a little chat about the news that his own mare had given birth to a little foal, I stepped back into the sunshine. On the way back to Main Street, where I'd told my mom I'd meet her, I bought an ice cream and sat down on a bench in the shade to wait for her.

Suddenly I saw something that made me do a double take. Right near where our car was parked was another car I recognized immediately: a blue pickup truck with a white trailer!

The truck's hood was up, and I saw the tall man with the checked shirt from the tack shop and another man, a little older with short hair, bending over the engine. I couldn't make out what they were saying, but I saw the older man pointing at some part of the engine, and he looked pretty worked up.

Suddenly a shiver went down my spine as I realized that it was these two that had been after Fireflight, and here I was, calmly sitting and licking an ice-cream cone in front of two genuine horse thieves. It seemed kind of unreal, but at the same time it was a frightening thought.

What was so amazing was that these two men looked like a couple of ordinary guys. In books these shady characters are always ugly and you can tell right away they're up to no good. But these two just looked like two guys standing in front of a car staring at a broken engine.

My throat was completely dry from nerves, and I tried to tell myself I was making it all up. It could just as easily have been another car with a trailer. And I'd only seen the first one from a distance, this morning in the woods. Maybe Mike was right when he'd said that somebody had just lost their way on the way to the riding school only a couple of miles away.

But then I had to think of the halter. Had they maybe just tried to get Fireflight in the trailer using just a rope and when that broke they decided to try again with a new halter? Or maybe Fireflight had resisted them so violently that he broke the halter that they had? That was sort of logical too.

The same had happened to my father and I years ago, when Fandango was still young and rambunctious. We wanted to go home after a competition. Fandango shied backwards when we tried to get him into the trailer and, in no time, he'd pulled the halter to shreds. We had to run after him through the parking lot full of other cars, trailers, and horses. I still turn red thinking about it, I was so embarrassed!

I decided to call Mike, quickly got out my cell phone and punched his number, but at the same time I heard my mother's voice behind me saying, "Oh, there you are, Sara!"

I turned off my phone and stood up. I was irritated. It was so typical of my dear sweet mother to show up at just the wrong moment.

"Who were you calling just now?" my curious mother asked as we walked to the car. "I saw you holding your phone."

"Nobody," I answered curtly. "I just wanted to see if it was on or off so I wouldn't waste the batteries."

"That's smart of you," she said, nodding.

Right then I got a bright idea.

"I have to throw this away," I said showing her napkin from around my ice-cream cone.

Before she could say anything, I was headed for a trash can right next to the blue pickup.

I'm sure my mother must have been puzzled, because I walked right past another trash can. But I couldn't let this opportunity go by. I had something more important to do – I had to take down the license number of those crooks.

I threw away the napkin and strolled slowly over to the blue pickup. I could hear my heart pounding, and I broke out in a clammy sweat as I tried to get as close as I could. But I couldn't get a look at the license plate. The big guy was standing with his wide pants legs covering the license plate, and I couldn't see any numbers or letters at all.

Frustrated, I walked back to our car and got in. I should have known! It was never that way on TV! The heroine can always get a look at the license plate. I sighed softly, while I wondered why the stories in books have so little to do with reality.

As soon as we got home, I hurried to my room and called Mike on his cell phone. It rang and rang, and but nobody answered. I nervously tried the number again. These cell phone numbers are long and it's easy to make a mistake, I thought, but I'd been right the first time. Mike wasn't there.

I carefully laid the telephone on my night table. I wasn't sure what to do. Why didn't he answer? Could something have happened while I was in town?

I didn't know, but eventually it occurred to me that it was no use sitting at the edge of my bed worrying. I tried Mike's number one last time, but nobody was there, so I gave up.

It was now nearly 6 p.m. and, despite the ice cream, I was getting hungry. When I went into the kitchen there wasn't a trace of either anything to eat, or my parents. Annoyed, I went out to the garden, where my mother was at it again in the rose bed. She looked at me and smiled.

"What is it?" she asked sweetly.

"I'm really hungry," I moaned. "Aren't we going to eat soon?"

"No, remember, your dad and I are going over to George and Mia's for a barbecue," she answered and stood up. "But there's a pizza in the freezer. You can have that if you want."

I sighed and went back into the kitchen. I'd forgotten the whole barbecue thing. It would be ages before the pizza was ready. I didn't feel like waiting that long. So, instead, I made a couple of sandwiches and had a glass of milk, while I thumbed through an old horse magazine.

After my frugal dinner, I decided to go for a ride. Fandango and I could use the practice and, after all, I didn't have anything better to do.

Not much later I was riding Fandango into our small outdoor ring. He was wild with joy. I burst out laughing and stroked his neck. What a wonderful animal my pony was! He always was in a good humor and was even enthusiastic about practicing.

I found out quickly why he was so enthusiastic. The jumps that Sophia and Camigo had used yesterday were still set up so, of course, he thought we were going to jump too. That wasn't on the agenda today, although I would rather jump with him a thousand times more than work on dressage.

I took us easily through one figure after the other and tried to keep Fandango's movements smooth and lively, while I kept changing tempo and from straight lines to diagonals. It wasn't easy to concentrate this evening, because I kept wondering what was going on with Mike. Fandango could feel it, and would move unwillingly and stiffly or would put up resistance.

Soon we'd both worked up a sweat. Even though it

was evening, the sun was still high in the sky and from where we were, the dust seemed to form a wall around us.

A moment later I heard my father calling something to me from over by the fence, and I rode over to him.

"What are you doing?" he asked harshly, and I looked at him in surprise.

"I'm doing some dressage exercises," I answered. "Why?"

"You're mistreating that horse," he said, and I let out a sigh.

Now I would get a long sermon, I thought, about how I don't ride in the correct way and that's why Fandango was so stiff, and blah, blah, blah. I readily admitted that dressage was the foundation of riding. I got a litany of good advice that I hadn't asked for and, furthermore, had heard already a thousand times.

But my father didn't stop at the good advice tonight. He entered the ring, told me to dismount and mounted Fandango himself. Fandango turned his head and stared in astonishment at my father's long legs sticking way out under Fandango's belly. I giggled to myself. My father was going out to the barbecue and was wearing his good pants, a clean shirt, and nice shoes, and the worst thing was he wasn't wearing a cap.

"Here, take my cap," I called to him, but he shook his head.

"I'll just be on him for a minute," he said. "Mom and I are leaving soon. OK, old boy, show me a few things."

My father pressed his calves into Fandango's side, and the horse went into a trot. He shook his head in annoyance and flipped his tail back and forth. Apparently my father was both too tall and too heavy, in his opinion, and I had to laugh silently again. Even with my father, he wasn't doing any better than he had been with me, and I was so glad to see it!

"And now pay attention!" my father barked to me from the other side. "You've got to keep better control of him. Use your inside rein to…"

Just then my mother walked out, with quick steps and in a bad mood from the looks of it. She'd really gotten dressed up for the occasion and was wearing a flowery summer dress with a little white jacket and pretty sandals. When she saw my father, she called to him to get off the horse immediately.

"We really have to go now. We're already running late," she said, annoyed, as my father rode up to her on Fandango.

"What on earth are you doing?" she cried, and my dad looked guiltily at the ground.

"Er…I just wanted to show Sara a couple of things," he explained sheepishly. He then dismounted and gave me the reins. "I'll be right there."

"Oh, I'm sure you will!" blurted my mother, "And, as usual, we'll get there late, just because you had to do something that would only take a minute, and then another thing that just would take a minute… And now you'll stink like horse too! This was supposed to be a nice party."

"Come on now," my father tried to calm her down. "It isn't that bad. I only rode a couple of rounds."

Mom breathed in through her teeth and looked at me.

"Call us if you have any problems. I talked to Sophia

63

on the phone, and she promised me she'd be home by 11:30 p.m."

"OK, fine," I said. As I got back onto Fandango, I had the feeling my pony was heaving a sigh of relief.

"Come on, let's go," said my mother decisively.

"OK, OK." Dad stroked Fandango's muzzle. Then he looked me in the eyes. "Now, just do what I told you. Use the inside rein while you tighten the outside rein at the same time…"

"Are you coming or not?" called my mother even more urgently, and headed for the car.

My dad sighed and trudged behind her to the car, and I put Fandango into a trot, holding the reins loosely. It was clear to me that once the car was out of sight, I'd hit the woods. I had absolutely no more interest in practicing dressage.

The woods were beautiful as they can only be on an early summer evening. The sun's rays streamed through the branches and there was that pleasant smell of horse, summer, and forest. I took in deep breaths, enjoying it intensely, and gave Fandango free rein. It seemed like he preferred this to that boring old ring too.

Suddenly I had an idea. I could try out the new jump!

I hadn't quite summoned up enough courage yet, so I decided to ride up to it and get a closer look first.

I don't know if Fandango was reading my mind, but he turned towards the obstacle course all by himself, and I shortened the reins. He started to canter with long smooth steps, and I felt the tension in my stomach increasing. Of course we were only going to look at the new jump, but somehow…

Presently the first jumps came into view. Fandango took the sight of them as an invitation, but I kept the reins tight and tried to keep him calm. He shook his head excitedly back and forth, and resisted my grip but I forced him to listen and do what I wanted.

I had to think back to when we'd just bought him, a few years ago. Fandango was only 5 years old then, but already big and strong. Even though he was a pony and only 14 hands high at the withers, he looked like a big horse with his strong neck, short back, wide croup, strong legs, and long fetlocks. The family we'd bought him from assured us he was a pure Connemara from Ireland, but that they'd only been too lazy to register him. My father and I, however, thought he was a cross, maybe between a Connemara and some cold-blooded breed.

Fandango, like Camigo, had been a lot darker when he was younger. His head was almost black, as were his mane, tail, and legs. The rest of his body was dark chestnut brown. For me it was love at first sight.

He seemed not to have had the best upbringing a horse could have, and it took a while before we knew just where we stood with each other. Back then I didn't have a lot of authority when it came to jumping, but since then he'd gotten more obedient and I'd grown stronger. That constant practice must have had an effect, although I had my doubts now and then.

After a little bend in the path, there was a long straight stretch where the new jump was. Fandango lifted his hooves and measured the oxer with careful eyes. He was definitely surprised to find a new obstacle here, where he was used to running full out, but he trotted over to it like a good boy and sniffed at the top beam.

Seen from horseback, the jump looked less daunting and I could feel the desire to jump conquering my fear. We could just try the hurdle out. Why not? We trotted back a little and I turned Fandango towards the oxer. He understood right away what I wanted and threw his head back and forth, while he pushed off with his back legs and flew to meet the jump. I realized this was all going too fast, but I couldn't stop him, so I let him go his way. He was experienced enough to estimate the distance and determine how he should take the jump. We had done even higher jumps in practice, and I had absolute faith in his strength in jumping.

But suddenly something completely unexpected occurred. Deep in between the trees I saw a flash of brown right in front of us. A deer, I realized. Fandango was three or four paces from the jump when the deer popped up before us and, like us, was very startled.

Fandango threw his head in the air, reared up and jumped to the side. I was thrown out of the saddle in a wide arc. The sky, ground, and trees all flew past me, and it seemed like an eternity before I hit the ground with such a force that I felt all the wind knocked out of me.

I lay still and stared at the blue summer evening sky over my head. My whole body hurt and my head was pounding so much that I almost couldn't see. I was afraid I'd never be able to get up again, and suddenly my head was filled with thoughts of paraplegia, wheelchairs, concussions, and other horrible things.

Eventually I tried to move anyway, and I was surprised to find I could sit up, as long as I did it carefully and slowly. I looked around me, glad to be alive.

The poor frightened deer was certainly miles away by now. Fandango was peacefully taking a little walk along the path to the edge of the road. He'd figured out that the brown apparition was only a silly deer and not some horse-eating monster. There was some tasty-looking plant life at the edge of the path he seemed to be exploring.

I worked my way up to a standing position and determined that at least I hadn't broken my legs. But when I tried to walk over to Fandango, my right knee was killing me. He looked at me with surprise as I limped towards him.

He stood there chewing on a few blades of grass. I called him affectionately, but – it would have to be this way – he didn't respond, and didn't want to be caught. Instead of coming towards me he walked away, so I couldn't grab the reins hanging from his bridle. Any second now, he could trip over them. In the gentlest voice I could muster I murmured all the cuss words I could think of, while I stumbled after him.

"Come on, Fandango. I'll give you a whole bucket of oats when we get home," I tried, but Fandango just stared at me with no interest whatsoever. Maybe my clever pony could tell I was lying to him, because he sauntered even farther away from me. He took another few leaves from a bush, went to stand next to it, and kept an eye on me while contemplatively chewing what he'd bitten off.

"Sweetie," I coaxed him, "don't you want to come over here next to me? Don't you, honey?"

But Fandango only sniffed and took a couple more leaves off the bush before changing to grass. He kept watching me, not wanting me to come too close.

Just then a cheery tune came from somewhere on the path. It was my cell phone! I'd totally forgotten that I'd had it with me. I must have lost it when I fell, but since it was ringing away it must have survived the fall. What should I do? Should I let Fandango stand there while I answered it, or should I keep up this stupid hunt for my stupid pony?

I ended up running – for what it was worth – to my phone, which was lying next to the path. Just as I reached it, it stopped ringing, but I could see on the display that it was Mike's number. I quickly picked it up, seized up with pain as I bent my knee, and called Mike.

"Hello!" said Mike, and I felt a warm glow spread through my body when I heard his voice.

"I just tried to call you," he continued enthusiastically. "I talked with the post office and the package delivery service in town, and I know for sure that whoever called this morning was trying to trick us. There's no package for Hans and neither one of them called here about a delivery. Anyway, they always send out a notice. So it was probably those horse thieves that called us, and they wanted to get me away from the house for a little while."

"Of course," I answered and felt my stomach go tight. "That also explains why they were out on that road so early this morning. They thought you'd be going right away to get that package, so they'd have all the time they needed to steal Fireflight."

"Exactly," Mike agreed. "Hey, what are you doing right now?"

"I'm standing here in the woods," I replied.

"In the woods?" he repeated in surprise. "Why?"

"Because my horse threw me from the saddle and now thestupid idiot won't let me catch him," I bleated, and I was suddenly aware I was closer to crying than laughing.

It all just seemed so awful all of a sudden. My knee hurt really badly, my head was spinning, and Fandango was still walking along the road far away from me. I didn't want to think about my pony disappearing in the trees and losing his way. The woods were gigantic, and there were swamps and deep ravines he could fall into.

When I started to think about all these dangers I felt the tears welling up in my eyes, but I tried to keep my voice steady so Mike wouldn't know I was in such bad shape.

"Oh," said Mike, who sounded concerned. "Should I come help you? Are you very far from here?"

"But you can't leave the house," I answered, trying to swallow the lump in my throat. "Then you'd leave Fireflight all alone."

Mike laughed.

"No, that's all settled."

"What?" I cried out. "Did the old guy come pick him up?"

"No, I thought of another way. You have to know…"

Just at that moment I felt something poking my back so hard I almost fell on my face. When I turned around,

Fandango was standing in front of me, looking like the most obedient pony in the world, and who would never do anything remotely wrong. I quickly made a grab for the reins and he let me take them without a complaint. He was being as meek as a lamb, and if he didn't look so innocent and if I wasn't so relieved I would have let him go and shouted at him to get lost and go drown himself in the nearest swamp.

"I just got a hold of Fandango again," I said to Mike and took a deep breath to get a hold of myself.

"Great," said Mike. "Go home and rest up. I'll call you later."

"OK, talk to you later," I answered and noticed that despite all the horrible things that had happened I had a pleasant tingling feeling.

In a little while I was able to get back in the saddle, then Fandango trotted calmly back home, looking like he didn't have a mischievous bone in his body. With a sigh of relief I dismounted right in front of the stable door and led him to his stall. When I'd unsaddled him, I got Camigo from the paddock and gave the two of them some oats and straw for the evening, before stumbling over to the house.

With difficulty I climbed the couple of stairs and opened the outside door of our sun porch. Or rather, I grabbed the door handle, but it wouldn't budge. Irritated, I struggled back down and around the house to try the kitchen door. No luck here either. Mom must have locked everything securely before they went off to George and Mia's.

I lifted the big flat stone by the stairway next to the

kitchen to get the spare key which was always under it, but there was no key. Suddenly I remembered that it was I who had used it last time, when I'd come back from town and nobody was home. I'd opened the door and hung up the spare key in the hallway, because I was too lazy to go back outside and put it back.

Enraged, I stared at our white house, locked up and silent. All the windows were dark and it was radiating the message, "Nobody home here!"

I did my best to stay calm, felt the tears suddenly coming, this time out of anger and despair. What could I do now?

Totally dejected, I sat down on the lowest step. My knee hurt and although my head wasn't ringing so badly any more, I still felt pretty miserable after my spectacular fall.

I was also in a terrible mood because all my plans had gone up in smoke. I'd actually been imagining how I'd come home nice and relaxed. Then I'd talk with Mike again, and have a nice long shower, because of course I hoped he wanted to see me this evening. He'd sounded that way when he said we'd talk later.

And look at me now, I thought, filthy from my head to my toes, sweaty and exhausted, in a ruined sweater and an old pair of riding pants that were already patched in a couple of places.

I ran my hands over my face and felt something sticky on my fingers. I must have gotten a good scratch above my eyebrows and it was still bleeding, I thought grumpily, and looked down at my blood-smeared fingertips.

Suddenly I had an idea. Behind the house there was a ladder. If I got it, I might be able to climb up onto the balcony and I could get in through the balcony door – that was always unlocked. Relieved, I stood up. I felt somewhat better, now that I'd found a solution and didn't have to sit around feeling bad.

I limped around the house and tried to see if the balcony door was open or not, and my mood went as sour as a minute ago. The balcony door was tightly locked up too, and there wasn't a single window open anywhere that I could see. I walked around the house one more time but it didn't change a thing – everything was closed and locked. I simply couldn't understand what my mother could have been thinking. Day and night, any time, there was always a window somewhere wide open, but of course not tonight.

I heard the familiar melody of my cell phone and picked up on the first ring. It was my mother.

"Hello, sweetie-pie!" she warbled. I could only manage a sour "hello".

"Dad and I decided we'd stay the night here," she said. "George and Mia suggested it, so we wouldn't have to drive home late tonight."

I sighed a very deep sigh.

"But I'm locked out! Can one of you come back and open the door for me? Then you can drive right back."

Mom was silent for a moment.

"Well," she said hesitantly, "we've both been drinking wine and it's not a good idea to drive. But won't Sophia be home soon?"

"No, she won't be home until 11:30 p.m. Remember, you told her yourself," I answered. "What will I do all night?"

Mom was silent again. Then I heard her talking with Dad, and a few seconds later he took the phone from her.

"What do you mean you're locked out? Isn't the spare key there?" he asked, and I explained why it wasn't.

"We can't come home now. Neither one of us should drive and a taxi would cost a fortune to come all the way there and back here. You'll just have to learn to watch out better for things like that," he said in his preachy voice and my face got even surlier, if that was possible.

Now Mom was back on the phone.

"Call Alexandra. Tell her to tell Sophia to come back right away and open the door for you," she said. "She'll just be a few minutes on the bike. They're probably sitting watching the video."

I almost blew it and told her that Sophia had gone to the movies in town, when I remembered that neither my mother nor my father knew anything about it, and I shut my mouth just in time. I already could see that my fate for this evening was to sit for hours waiting outside, while my little sister was having fun at the movies and my parents were enjoying themselves with their friends at the barbecue.

"We have to go now," said my mother. "Call if there's a problem. Love you, honey!"

The connection was broken with a click. I sat down again with a sigh. I was feeling really sorry for myself, and it didn't feel very good at all. The sun was just going down, the mosquitoes were getting ready to attack, and I had no idea what to do next. At last I stood up and stumbled towards the stable. Maverick came to the gate when I walked past the paddock. I took him inside so he wouldn't get devoured by the mosquitoes and bloodthirsty horseflies. He didn't have a halter, so I led him by

74

his forelock. I actually could have let him walk by himself, because he was walking very deliberately towards his stall. It was a pleasure to not have to coax the horses in using cuss words for once.

I laid fresh straw in his stall and gave him some more hay to eat. Then I limped to the water spigot. I wanted to get a good look at my injured knee. I was able to take off my boots and riding pants without too much pain. Then I examined my knee, which was completely blue and red, and all scraped and swollen. I moistened a cotton rag and dabbed at the broken skin. Then I took a little bit of the iodine ointment we normally used for the horses, and smeared it on the wounds. It burned like anything and it brought tears to my eyes, but I knew it would keep the wounds from getting infected, so I didn't mind. This was the way it was, I thought, and threw the rag on the manure pile.

I put a bandage on my knee and went to the tack room and took a length of elastic, which was really meant for Fandango. I carefully bound my knee with the fluorescent green ribbon. It wasn't exactly high fashion, but I already felt better having taken my riding pants off and cleaned up my wounds.

Fandango was following everything I did looking interested. He must have been wondering why I was limping. It wouldn't have surprised me if he'd called the vet to come and give me injections and more ointments if he could have.

I limped over to him in his stall and stroked his neck. After all, it wasn't his fault that that deer popped up in front of us. It was really my fault, because I'd decided to jump over the oxer even though we were all alone in the woods.

I leaned against Fandango with my eyes closed and felt how much my whole body hurt. I'd also discovered a new scrape on my arm, my shoulders ached, and I wasn't sure if I'd be able to get out of bed the next day. I wasn't even sure I could get into bed at all tonight. If not, I would have no choice but to spend the night in the barn covered with a horse blanket. At least I wouldn't freeze on such a nice warm night, I thought soberly, and heard my stomach start to growl.

I walked to the tack room and dived into an old cupboard we had there. I found a bottle of fruit juice that was still good and some dry cookies. I took them to the stable and sat down on a bale of straw. Once I'd emptied the bottle, I thought of calling Mike.

Just then I saw the latch of the stable door slowly moving. There was somebody outside! Somebody was trying to sneak into the stable!

I was terrified and jumped off the straw bale, staring at the door and getting even more frightened by the second. My heart was in my throat and my legs felt like jelly. I limped as quickly as I could to the manure fork over by the straw bales.

I would defend myself against the intruder, whoever it was.

Grimly I stared at the door as it opened with a creak.

A couple of seconds later Mike stuck his head around the door. I stared at him with my mouth open. I dropped the fork and Mike looked at me, totally confused.

"What are you doing?" he asked and looked first at

me, then at the fork, then back at me. "Are you going to clean out the stables now? And dressed like that?"

When I looked down, I understood his surprise. There I was, dirty, blood-smeared, my hair a mess, my sweater ripped, a fluorescent green bandage around my knee, and my feet and legs bare. I could have passed for something out of a horror movie.

"What are you doing here?" I asked in a trembling voice. "You really scared me! I thought it was the horse thieves."

Mike started to laugh.

"Come on! I was just worried about you. You weren't answering your cell phone. I must have tried you 10 times, the last time was about a half hour ago."

I stared at my cell phone on the bale of straw and felt the heat rising in my cheeks. After talking to my mother I'd felt so pessimistic I'd turned it off.

"It, um, wasn't on," I mumbled, embarrassed.

But that didn't seem to worry Mike anymore. Instead he looked at me with concern in his eyes.

"My God, you look like a mess. What happened, anyway?"

I told him what had happened with our attempt to try the new jump, trying to keep it brief, and when it was over Mike wasn't sure whether to laugh or feel sorry for me.

"And guess what else? I'm locked out," I finished.

"Why don't you come with me?" asked Mike tenderly. "You can have a shower, and I can lend you some clothes. You can't walk around like that – you'll scare people to death."

"And how am I supposed to get there?" I asked and sighed. "I can't walk or bike that far, and I don't exactly feel like riding Fandango right now."

Mike was thinking as he looked around our little stable.

"How's that cinnamon pony?" he asked, pointing to Maverick. "Can you ride him?"

"Of course. But he doesn't have a saddle right now. It's in the shop."

"Well, can't you ride without one? He can hang out in one of our empty stalls."

I nodded. It was a good idea. My whole body hurt, and I didn't really feel like spending the evening in the stable staring at the walls. Mike's suggestion sounded really great, and the best thing about it was that he'd thought it up himself.

I put Maverick's halter on and led him outside, and got on his old back with a little help from Mike. My knee still hurt, but with the weight off my leg it felt a lot better. This would be fine.

What I was worried about was that I was so dizzy and didn't really feel well. My head had taken a heavy blow, and I was wondering if I might have a slight concussion.

I pressed my dusty and dilapidated cap tighter to my head and it occurred to me that at least some good would come out of today: I'd probably get a nice new cap.

Actually, you should never wear a cap if you've had an accident in it. But in this case I didn't have any other choice and a cap full of holes offered more protection than none.

I took Maverick's reins, and we rode slowly over the road to Hans and Maggie's farm. I peeked over at Mike, who was riding an ancient, rattling woman's bike, and I felt shivers go through my body. I was well on my way to falling in love with him. No, I thought, it's best not to let it show. I'm sure he's 18, maybe even 19. He'd never be interested in a girl so much younger than he is. I let out a sigh.

"Is something the matter?" asked Mike and looked up at me. "Are you in pain?"

"Yes," I answered quickly, so he'd think that that was why I'd sighed like that, but the pain in my knee and my head together were no match for the pain in my heart. Of course I didn't have a chance, making a friend who I was also in really love with.

At Hans and Maggie's the stable was silent and empty, and I looked curiously around me.

"Where's Fireflight?" I asked. "Did you put him in the paddock?"

"He's not here any more," Mike explained with a grin, while I took off Maverick's halter. "A friend of mine and I brought him to another stable this afternoon. I didn't think it was a good idea to keep him here."

"Why not?" I asked. "Has something else happened?"

Mike nodded.

"Early this afternoon, when I had to leave the farm to get something. I'd locked Fireflight in the stable, and I drove out to the gas station near the freeway. I couldn't have been gone longer than a half an hour, probably less, but while I was gone somebody tried to break into the stable. There were marks around the lock, as if somebody had tried to force it with a crowbar, and a window in back was broken. It was only luck that nobody climbed inside."

I cleared my throat.

"Was anyone here when you got back? Or did you see any other cars on the way?"

Mike shook his head.

"No, nobody, and there wasn't anyone around here when I got back."

"They either drove away straight from here," I suggested, "or they took the old road through the woods again. They could have parked back there and walked over here. When they heard you coming back, they ran away through the woods."

Mike nodded.

"By the way, Hans has an aerial photo of the farm hanging in his office," he said. "I took a look at it. You can see that road pretty clearly on it, so it's not like nobody knows about it."

That afternoon I'd been in town and had seen those guys in the parking lot. I told Mike about seeing one of them buying a halter and then the two of them standing by the car looking under the hood. Like me, he wondered how it all fit together.

Maverick seemed not to object to being in a stranger's stable. He looked interestedly around and began to sift through the straw for something edible. Mike made a last check of the stable, then shut and locked all the doors, while I gave Maverick some hay to chew on. Then he turned out the light, and we went to Mike's room.

"I hope they don't kidnap Maverick by mistake," I said, half joking and half sincerely, as we entered the hallway.

"Nahhhh," laughed Mike, "why would they do that? OK, he's the same color as Fireflight. But if they can't tell your father's retired crossbreed from a thoroughbred, then we're not exactly talking about professional horse thieves."

"I have to tell you that my father will personally kill anyone who harms a hair on old Maverick's head! I'm serious," I said with a chuckle.

81

"I solemnly swear, your majesty, to defend Maverick with my life if anything should happen," said Mike very ceremoniously. We both had a good laugh.

Mike presented me with the tiniest bathrobe I'd ever seen. Then he gave me a big towel, along with a clean pair of jeans and a sweater that I could borrow.

"And please take that ridiculous horse bandage off your knee," he concluded. "I must have a normal ace bandage around here somewhere. I'll go look for one."

He showed me to the bathroom and shut the door for me. I looked at myself in the mirror over the little sink, and had to laugh. I really looked awful! There was a long scratch over my eyes, my hair was going every which way and I was dirty and sweaty. You can imagine what a blessing it was to get under a hot shower and feel the water streaming over my aching body. It did hurt when the hot water touched my knee, but I felt a lot better when I was finished.

The jeans and sweater that Mike had lent me were much too big, but I turned up the sleeves and the cuffs and they looked better already. I combed my hair, and before going into the kitchen I made a silly face in the mirror and grinned.

In the kitchen I could smell freshly-made coffee. I went to sit at the table and Mike handed me a steaming mug. Only then did I notice how my head was beginning to spin. I was afraid I might pass out. Maybe it would be better just to lie down. On the other hand I knew I'd feel better if I could eat something.

"How's your knee?" asked Mike with genuine concern. "Does it still hurt a lot?"

"It already feels better. I just feel a little dizzy." Mike looked alarmed.

"You're dizzy? If you think you might have had a concussion you ought to go to the doctor."

"Oh no," I said, trying to drop the subject and feeling bad that I'd even mentioned it. "I'm sure it's nothing."

"Want a bandage for your knee?" asked Mike and I nodded.

"Let me put it on right now," I said. "If that's OK with you."

"Of course! Go ahead," answered Mike and he put two pieces of bread in the toaster. "How about a cheese sandwich? Or two?"

"I'll start with one," I said carefully, because although I felt really hungry, I wasn't sure I could actually get anything down with this dizziness.

Thank God Mike hadn't noticed any of this, because he started to tell me about all he'd done today. First he'd called the post office, and then the police. He'd talked to an officer and told her everything.

She had agreed that it looked like someone was after Fireflight. Unfortunately, the police couldn't do a lot to help Mike. Fireflight had come back, after all. It was only a question of who had broken the gate. And it wasn't a crime to drive a car and horse trailer on a dirt road.

The phone call he'd gotten this morning was certainly meant to lure him away from the house, but Mike couldn't tell her who had called, and it was too late to find out.

Mike had asked if the police could keep an eye on the farm, so they could catch the thieves in the act, but the police officer had laughed heartily. The police couldn't even begin to think about doing that, she'd said, because they had so few people to cover a large territory. But if the men were to come back, then Mike should just call and they'd come right away, she'd said.

After talking with the policewoman, Mike made a decision. Fireflight had to get away from here, and right now. He'd called Hans and told him the whole story, and Hans agreed it was a good idea to move him. Now Fireflight was at a stable about 20 miles away, and Mike seemed very relieved that he was gone.

Mike had turned off the ceiling light, and lit an old hurricane lamp and a couple of candles. We sat in the tiny kitchen and talked about Fireflight for a while, and gradually started talking about other things.

Mike had already done a lot of exciting things in his life, even though he wasn't even 19. After high school he'd taken courses in horse training, and he'd traveled around taking care of a few jumpers. He'd also competed himself, while he was still in high school. I'd thought about studying horse training, but there was no place around here where you could take courses like that.

Several times this evening, it occurred to me, I had to admit that talking with Mike seemed really natural and conversation just flowed by itself. Even though we'd only just met, it felt like we'd known each other forever, and later on he would say the same thing about this evening. If I hadn't had such a headache it would have been perfect!

We talked and talked. You know how time flies when you're having fun. I'd told Mike that my sister would be home at 11:30 p.m., but even though we were checking the clock, it was almost midnight when we stood up.

"Well, my sister ought to be back by now," I said.

"And if she isn't, come back here. You can sleep on the couch," responded Mike a little shyly.

I blushed and looked down at the floor, hoping he hadn't seen. If he did, he would surely know I had no experience with boys.

We walked outside into the balmy summer night. The sun had been down for a while, but there was still a little light on the horizon and the sky was a gorgeous dark blue. I could just see two deer grazing at the edge of a field. The sweet smell of the jasmine around the house was intense and sweet in the air, and everything was incredibly still and beautiful. I knew at that moment that I'd remember this evening all my life.

I walked clumsily to the stable with Mike. My headache was a little better now, and I wasn't feeling so dizzy either. In the stable, Maverick was standing up looking like he'd been napping. When he saw us coming, he lifted up his head and looked at us sleepily. We didn't turn on the light, since there was still some light outside.

Mike opened the door of the stall and Maverick turned his ears back right away. He looked as if he was asking, "What do you want? Can't you see I'm sleeping?" He yawned so wide you could see all his old yellowed teeth.

Mike laughed and stroked his neck.

"Are you tired, sir?" he asked. "Come on, you'll be home in no time, and you can sleep in your own bed."

Then Mike looked at me and this time I was able to return his gaze without dropping my eyes to the ground. He smiled at me, and you could almost say that he looked a little shy.

"It was great talking with you," he said a little cautiously, and I felt myself blushing again.

I was glad it was so dark in the stable, so Mike couldn't see how red my face was. I didn't know what to say to him, but eventually I said it was nice talking to him too.

"And there's something else I wanted to ask you," Mike continued. I felt my heart start to pound, because his voice had a really different tone now, one that went all the way into my bones.

But just when he wanted to say the words that I was hoping he'd say, my cell phone started to ring. Three guesses who it was.

It was of course my sister – who else would be calling so late? With a sister like that, who needed enemies? She was amazing!

"What?" I asked impatiently, and for the first time, my sister was a little bit bashful.

"We missed the bus!"

"You what?" I almost screamed into the phone.

"Missed the bus," Sophia answered sheepishly. "What'll we do now? There's no way to get home!"

"Yes there is, you're going to walk," I said indignantly. "It's only 10 miles. If you hurry, you'll be home by sunup!"

"Are you crazy?" screamed Sophia. "Hey, are Mom and Dad home yet?"

"You are so lucky," I snapped. "They're staying over at George and Mia's."

I heard my sister let out a sigh of relief, but then Alexandra got on the phone.

"Are you with Mike?" she asked, in as shy a tone as Sophia had just had. "Couldn't he come get us? He has a car, doesn't he?"

"Of course he can't!" I answered, annoyed. "How can you ask such a dumb question. You know I can't ask him to do something like…"

Mike looked at me inquisitively, and I raised my eyes to the sky. "You stupid idiots! Why couldn't you just have watched the time and made the last bus?"

"Please Sara, can't you just ask him?" begged Alexandra who sounded like she'd burst into tears any minute. "My parents will have a fit if I don't get home right away," she said, "and I've told them that I was going to your house. They didn't know we were in town with my brother and his friends."

"So you both lied to your parents?" I exclaimed. "You're just getting what you deserve."

"I know, but the movie lasted longer than we thought and so we… well, we just forgot," whined Alexandra and started to sob.

I sighed and tried to think of a way out of this annoying situation, but my head was spinning.

"Can I talk with them a second?" asked Mike and took the phone from my hand.

I unwillingly gave it to him, and he had a couple of words with Alexandra. Then he said "OK, I'll be there in 15 minutes. You two stay right there at the bus stop and don't go anywhere."

I stared at him. I couldn't believe he really was going to go to town and pick them up. Mike gave me back my cell phone.

"I feel sorry for them," he said looking amused. "I was young and foolish once too. And anyway, you can't get into the house without your sister's key, right?"

I nodded. I'd forgotten about the key. Good thing one of us had a clear head.

"Take Maverick and ride home. I'll drop your sister off soon."

I nodded. The very special mood that had passed between us, had vanished into thin air. Now Mike's voice sounded back to normal again, and he purposefully walked out of the stable. A little later I heard a car start up and drive away. He stepped on the gas so hard I heard gravel flying away under the tires.

I stumbled down the hall in the stable to get Maverick's halter, which was hanging from a hook. We'd really had a nice evening, I thought, and I gave a little silly laugh in the near darkness. This night was worth a lot to me.

When I walked into Maverick's stall with the halter, he approached me with his ears pricked up. I still hadn't turned on a light, because there was still enough light to see by and I put his halter on with no problems.

Just as I stroked Maverick's long ears, I saw the headlights of a car coming over the gravel driveway. I couldn't believe Mike would be back already. I went to the window to get a look.

But then a shiver went down my spine. It wasn't Mike's white car, but the big blue pick-up with the white trailer. The horse thieves! Where could I hide quickly?

The first thing I thought of was that I had to lock the stable door. I walked to it and turned the key twice in the lock. My legs were shaking so much I thought I wouldn't be able to walk, but I made it to the stall. I opened the door and went in to Maverick while I tried to force myself to think. Why did people in detective stories always seem so cool-headed and brave? I was scared to death. My heart was beating so hard and fast that it almost hurt.

I remembered that I still had my cell phone with me. I quickly got it and tried Mike's number, but nothing happened. I tried another few times, but I got nothing. I checked the batteries and now, when I really, really needed this phone to work, it seemed they were dead. There was no way I could reach either Mike or the police.

In despair I watched the car and trailer come down the driveway and stop in front of the stable. I heard the car doors shut and a voice say something. Just seconds later somebody came to the stable door and tried to open it. My throat was dry as dust and I had never been so scared in my life.

"That damn boy's locked up the horses!" said an angry voice.

The other one said something I couldn't understand and immediately afterwards I heard one of the car doors shut.

"I wonder if there are even any horses at all in there?" asked the other guy as he shone a flashlight in through the window.

I ducked down behind the stall wall so they wouldn't see me. But Maverick was staring curiously towards the window, and I heard one of the men say that the horse was in the stable. They tried to open the door again. So it was the same two that had already tried to break in once today.

They rattled at the door. Then there was a scratching,

awful noise from the keyhole. I stared at the door, and suddenly I could think clearly again! It was clear to me that they'd be inside in a matter of seconds, and who knows what they'd do if they found me and Maverick there. I didn't want to think about what they'd do to our sweet old horse. I couldn't let that happen! But how could we get away?

I had a flash – the back door, of course! All the way back in the stable, near where Maverick was, there was a small door to freedom, near the manure pile. From there it was only a short distance to the woods and once we were safely in the shelter of the trees, we could hide, because I knew those woods like the back of my hand.

I heard the men still fiddling with the lock. Time after time they jerked on the door, bashed at it, and swore dreadfully. They were so involved with what they were doing that they probably wouldn't notice if we escaped. I realized I didn't have much more time if our escape were to succeed.

Quickly I led Maverick to the hall. Luckily he wasn't shod, so his hooves didn't make any noise at all. He was also a clever horse, and he walked soundlessly. Maybe he could feel how serious a situation this was. Maverick was an intelligent old horse, and I had felt many times before that he could read minds.

I tried to open the back door. It was locked, but the key was in the lock so I turned it carefully. The slightest sound could have been enough to alert those criminals and then they'd be right at the back door and the game would be over.

Hans was always fastidious about his work, and he

kept everything in perfect working order. The lock was well oiled and opened easily, as did the door itself. Cautiously I led Maverick outside, around the manure pile and to the narrow cement edge around the manure pile. I climbed quickly onto it and was about to jump on Maverick's back, when a loud voice came from a corner of the stable.

"He's riding away with the horse! Come back!"

He? Oh, of course – they thought I was Mike. Apparently one of the guys had walked around the building and discovered Maverick and me.

Maverick was frightened by the sudden yelling and gave a start to the side. My attempt to jump on his back half failed and I landed on my stomach hanging over his back. Panicking, I tried to get myself up to a sitting position, but Maverick had already started trotting towards the woods. He clearly had had enough of all this and wanted to get home as fast as he could.

"Stop!" yelled the guy, and I heard him panting as he ran after us. He had almost caught up to us, when I was able to throw my right leg over Maverick's back and sit up straight. My knee hurt so badly that it brought tears to my eyes. Maverick went into a strange and uneasy trot, swinging me back and forth. I nearly fell off the whole time, but I was able hold onto his mane to stay on. We were only a little way from the woods, when the other thief appeared on the other side. He wanted to cut us off and since he was faster and braver than his comrade, he quickly reached where we were. He ran to Maverick's head and tried to grab the reins.

"Whoa!" he yelled.

Maverick wasn't about to obey this creep. He threw himself to the side so the guy couldn't grab him, to Maverick's delight, but not to mine. His sudden shift made me start to slide off him. I desperately tried to cling to him, but when he began to gallop I lost hold of him. I bounced all over his back and slowly but surely sank toward the ground. I tried to hold on for dear life, but there was no more saving me. When Maverick jumped over a little ditch right before the edge of the woods, I flew through the darkness and landed with a thud on the ground. Around me everything went black.

The next thing I could remember was someone shining a bright flashlight right in my face. Annoyed, I put my arm up to my face to block the light and sputtered to the flashlight's owner to please not tie me up.

"Idiot," I heard someone say, "what did you want with that horse? Good thing we caught up with you! But – it's a girl!"

"A girl?" I heard another voice say. "Where did she come from? There was only supposed to be a guy here."

Dizzily I tried to sit up, but everything started to spin again in my head.

"Just stay there," said the one with the flashlight. "Are you all right? Did you hurt yourself?"

"I'm just a little dizzy," I answered and noticed the ground underneath me seemed to be moving.

It was actually pretty weird that a shady character was standing in front of me making sure I was all right instead of putting a gun to my head or something. When my eyes got used to the darkness, I recognized the old guy with the short hair who I'd seen that afternoon (it seemed like ages ago!) in the parking lot.

"What the devil were you doing on top of that horse,"

snarled the other man, and I turned my head towards him. It was the tall guy with the checked short, holding on Maverick. "We were lucky that we could catch him," he continued. "You must know how much he's worth. This is a valuable show horse, not some pony you can just ride in circles."

"But that's not Fireflight," I said and tried my best to keep my voice steady. "That's Maverick."

"Aw, come on," sneered the guy holding Maverick. "Next you'll be telling us that Little Red Riding Hood is out there in the woods."

"It's true," I said, feeling the tears burn my eyes. "This horse is my father's."

"Yeah, right," said the guy with the flashlight. At least he sounded a little friendlier. "Why don't you try and get up now?"

I was able to stand up, and we all walked back towards the farm. I felt sick and unable to think clearly at all.

What were these men planning to do with Maverick? And with me? Everything was so chaotic and confusing that I couldn't see any way out. I just couldn't think of anything smart.

When we got to the trailer, they let the door down. I tried desperately to stop them.

"But this is the wrong horse," I sobbed forlornly and tried to stop the big guy from putting a halter and bit on Maverick. "This is my father's horse. Let him go."

"Let's hope he doesn't make so much fuss getting in the trailer this time," the older one grunted.

"Naw, he's gentle as a little lambie now," answered the other. "And he's put on a few pounds too!"

"Well, he's just been sitting around for almost a week doing nothing," said the old guy, turning towards me. "By the way, this is really my horse. So I'll come and get him whenever I feel like it. Got that?"

"He's not yours!" I screamed, but I couldn't get out of his grasp.

Although the older guy was small and sinewy, he was strong as an ox and he held me so tightly that I thought my arm was in a vise. Meanwhile the other guy was leading Maverick to the horse trailer.

Maverick looked discouraged and I hoped with all my heart that he would refuse to go up the ramp. I knew he could put up a good fight now and then. But usually he was very good-natured, and seemed like it now, even though this situation should have been really strange for him.

A second later he walked with heavy steps up the ramp and into the trailer.

I was past despair. Maverick! These men intended to take Maverick with them, but what would they do when they discovered they'd made a mistake and taken the wrong horse? I didn't dare think about it.

I let the tears come and between sobs, tried to explain that Fireflight wasn't here at all, but the two men seemed not to care. The big guy closed the trailer up and jumped into the cabin of the pick-up. When I heard the engine start and saw the taillights of the trailer go on, all my hope left me. The older one gave a me a friendly pat on my arm and said he'd call Hans up tomorrow. Then he jumped in the pickup and it slowly left the farm.

Completely exhausted, I dropped to the ground, put

my face in my hands and started to sob. I realized that now was the time to do something useful, like run inside and call the police, but my legs wouldn't obey me.

I sniffled and sobbed, and heard the sound of the pick-up's engine fade into the distance. Maverick was gone, maybe for-ever. Feeling hopeless, I kept crying, but I knew that despite how awful I felt, I had to call the police and tell them what was going on… but first I'd have to get into the house!

I had almost gotten all the way up when I suddenly saw the headlights of a car coming towards me. Could it be…?

It was! Instantly it seemed my lameness fell away, and I could move again. On shaky legs I walked over along the gravel path to where the pickup and trailer had come to a stop, where Mike's little white car had parked side-ways on the road and blocked the way for them. Mike was standing, arguing with the two men, and my sister was there too. She stared at them with no idea at all of what was going on.

I ran as best as I could over to them, and reached the group exactly at the moment that Mike said something very smart: "Maverick is not Fireflight and it's easy to prove!"

"How?" asked the big guy suspiciously.

"Fireflight is a stallion, right? And you've got a gelding there in your trailer."

The two men looked at each other in astonishment. Then the older one mumbled something and walked around the trailer to undo the ramp and lead Maverick out, so they could see if Mike was right. I was so happy

97

that tears streamed down my face as the thieves unloaded our old horse. As Mike looked on, still furious, the old guy walked back and forth with a flashlight, examining Maverick here and there. Then he let out a string of curse words that made my hair stand on end.

"Where's my horse?" he snarled angrily and shone the flashlight right in Mike's face.

"Not here anyway," answered Mike. "He's in a safe place. You see, someone tried to steal him, just like you warned me about on the phone."

"Who gave you permission to take him somewhere else?" growled the little old guy and waved his flashlight in the air.

"Hans said it would be all right," answered Mike calmly, "so please stop yelling. Why don't you tell me why you didn't call to tell me you were coming? And why show up like this in the middle of the night?"

"I called, but nobody picked up the phone," said the old one crabbily. "I'll pick up my own horse whenever I feel like it, you got that?"

I looked at Mike, then at the old guy and back at Mike.

So the old guy was Fireflight's owner. I just didn't understand any more. But I wasn't the only one, I thought, looking at my sister. She was staring at me wide-eyed, and I realized it would take me some time tonight to explain everything to her.

The old guy calmed down bit by bit and said curtly that he'd wanted to come and get Fireflight, because he wasn't sure whether or not Fireflight really would be safe with Mike. But first they'd had car trouble, and then they'd mistaken Maverick for Fireflight...and we knew the rest of the story. Mike listened patiently and when the old guy was finished making his case, things got really quiet. At last the old guy said, "I'll come back tomorrow, and I want my horse to be there. Understand? Now can you move your car or do we have to stand here all night?"

"Of course," said Mike with resignation. "What time do you think you'll come over?"

"I can't tell you for sure now," answered the old guy, irritated. "I'll call you before I come, though."

The old guy and his bigger comrade got in the truck and started the engine. Mike walked to his car to move it away, and my sister and I walked slowly towards home with Maverick. It was already starting to get light, the birds were singing and the sky was that shade of blue you only see after a really hot day.

"Now you really have to tell me what happened," said Sophia excitedly, once we were underway. "What were you and Mike doing there? I don't understand any of it."

"I'll tell you later," I answered, exhausted. "But first we're bringing Maverick home."

Luckily home was only a few hundred yards. My knee was hurting like mad, and I felt even more miserable than before. If I didn't get a concussion the first time, I thought, I surely got one just now when I fell off of Maverick.

When we got home, Sophia took Maverick to his stall, while I headed straight into the living room and carefully stretched out on the couch.

I had a pounding headache, was exhausted and shattered, and only wanted to do one thing: sleep. But that wasn't going to happen, because my sister came in just then, followed by Mike.

"Now you have to tell me everything," Sophia insisted. "Hey, who wants a cup of hot chocolate? I do."

"Sounds good," said Mike.

"I don't want anything," I answered and yawned for what felt like the millionth time.

Mike and Sophia went to the kitchen to make hot chocolate, while I stayed on the couch. When they came back in, I didn't feel like sitting up, and I didn't have the energy even if I'd wanted to. I felt like I was floating through the air and everything, including the couch, was colliding with moving walls.

Mike told her what had happened over the last few days, and for once my sister sat still and listened. The story of how Fireflight came to Hans totally unexpectedly, how he disappeared and reappeared, and how we'd discovered that someone had forced and opened the old gate, took a long time to tell.

Then Mike told her about the morning's telephone call from someone pretending to work at the post office, and the attempted break-in when he'd left the farm for just a short time. And last but not least was the remarkable fact that Fireflight's owner suddenly showed up in the middle of the night to come get his own horse.

The way Mike told it made it sound like a suspense movie. It was clear that my sister would really have loved to be in my shoes tonight during all the excitement.

"Great, guys," she complained as soon as Mike was finished with everything. "And you didn't tell me anything before! I could have helped you, you know, played lookout or something."

"Sure," I grumbled. "You would have been fantastic."

The sarcasm in my voice didn't go unnoticed by my sister. She looked at me with irritation as she sipped her hot chocolate. I looked at Mike.

"I just meant the whole thing's been insane from the beginning."

Mike nodded and smiled at me.

"You got that right."

Sophia raised her eyes to the ceiling.

"You guys don't get it," she said. "Fireflight's owner is still out there and is still planning to steal his own horse and have him disappear."

Mike and I looked at Sophia we both asked at the same time, "How do you know that?"

"Oh my God," she answered, shrugging her shoulders, "you just know! That's how it always goes in detective stories. He probably has money problems and so now he's trying to get the insurance money for Fireflight. But first the horse has to disappear mysteriously. That's why he stole Fireflight first from this out-of-the-way farm and next he'll take him from his ownstable."

Mike laughed.

"You've been reading too many detective stories," he said to Sophia, who was looking pretty insulted, now that neither one of us was taking her theory seriously.

"Even if it's as you say, it still sounds too impossible," Mike continued. "Things like that just don't happen in real life."

"Yeah, right," Sophia snapped, "How would you

know? But pay no attention to what I think. It was just a thought."

My head started to pound again, and I couldn't keep from yawning.

"I have to get to bed. I'm totally exhausted," I groaned.

"You look it," said Sophia, and there actually was something like sympathy in her voice.

She got up and brought the cups to the kitchen, and I stumbled behind Mike to the hall.

He was yawning and I was yawning, and we stood like that for a second, not knowing what to say to each other. Then I remembered something I wanted to ask him.

"There's something else I don't understand," I said to Mike. "What were Lind and his friend doing in the woods with their trailer so early in the morning?"

"Hm," said Mike, reflecting. "I think the guys that wanted to get Fireflight must have been keeping an eye on the farm. How else could they have known when I left to do a little shopping? And tonight was the same. I'd barely gone when the old guy and his friend showed up to get the horse. There's a good chance they saw me leave and figured there was nobody else at home."

"You mean Sophia might be right? That he's really trying to steal his own horse?" I asked cautiously.

"Yes," answered Mike, "and soon we'll find out if it's true. Tomorrow Fireflight's going back home and this whole thing will be over."

"Good," I agreed, and yawned again. "Oh, I'm so tired…"

"I can believe it. But aside from that, I think you were really brave," said Mike sweetly.

He was about to go, but turned back to face me and ran his hand gently over my cheek. Then he smiled a little shyly, while he went down the steps and got into his car. He started the engine, waved at me, stepped on the gas, and disappeared down the dirt road.

I stood there staring after him. My knee hurt, I was dizzy and my whole body ached, but, I thought happily, it was all worth it.

I slept until almost noon the next morning, when my mother knocked on the door asking if I was planning to get up so we could have lunch. I pulled on my green shorts and a big white T-shirt. It was really hot outside, and I was hot too. When I came into the kitchen and saw my mother's face, I realized I couldn't count on any approval for my choice appearance today. I wasn't looking forward to explaining why I looked so awful, with bruises all over, a long scratch on my forehead and a few other hefty scrapes, and why my knee was bandaged.

"Why, what happened to you?" asked my mother, and her tone of voice meant that she expected the truth, the whole truth, and nothing but the truth from me.

"What's the matter with your knee? And what a deep cut you have on your forehead!" she continued, looking very worried.

"I fell," I mumbled and poured a glass of juice. I was incredibly thirsty.

"A deer jumped in front of us, Fandango was startled and jumped aside, and I was thrown out of the saddle," I answered matter-of-factly, as if this sort of thing was completely normal and happened to me at least once a day.

104

"Oh really?" responded Mom and looked at me piercingly. "A deer? In the ring?"

"After you left, I went for a ride," I mumbled. "It was just too hot to do dressage."

"Honey, you know I don't like it if you go riding outside when there's nobody home. You could have been lying out in the woods all night."

I nodded, because she was right. That could have happened last night.

"I had my cell phone with me," I said, trying to talk my way out of trouble. "I could have called for help."

"That would be a little difficult if you were unconscious! Did you fall on your head or something?"

I nodded gingerly, because my neck and shoulders really hurt now. Just then my father came into the kitchen, holding my dented and stained cap, which I'd thrown in the hallway, and waved it in the air.

"What have you been up to?" he asked sternly. I thought this wasn't fair, because now it was two against one.

"She went out riding alone last night and got thrown from the saddle," said my mom. "We'd better talk seriously about this. I don't like it that Sara's going riding alone when nobody else is home."

My father nodded in agreement, and his face looked very stern.

"That wasn't very bright of you," he said disapprovingly. "What happened? By the looks of this helmet, you must have been going really fast!"

"We came onto a path and then suddenly a deer appeared and scared Fandango," I explained for the second time.

Dad looked threatening.

"I know, I know, and you let the reins go and were daydreaming. How many times do I have to tell you that you have to concentrate when you're riding and not let the horse just go where he wants?" I stared into my glass sheepishly, but I was thinking how lucky it was that Mom and Dad didn't know how fast I'd been going when that all happened.

Just then I felt really terrible, and I shoved my juice glass away. Everything around me started spinning and I had to hold onto the edge of the table so I wouldn't fall over.

"My poor honey, what 's the matter?" asked my mother worriedly. "Don't you feel well? Are you dizzy?"

The only sound I could get out was a "Yeah," and Mom looked at me with concern in her eyes.

"We've got to get you to the hospital! You've probably had a concussion!"

"But I had my cap on," I stammered in protest. "I'll be fine if I can just lie down for a little while."

But my mother wouldn't hear it.

"We're going to the emergency room. You're as white as a sheet, Sara. How do you feel now?"

"Not so good," I whispered, because that was the truth, and I had no more objections to getting in the car with her and going to town.

On the way over we ran into Hans and Maggie, in their big car. Maggie waved cheerily to us, while Hans just looked the other way. As tired as I was, it hit me that it would be harder for Mike and I to meet now that they were back home. But at that moment I didn't care because I felt so awful. I almost asked my mom to pull over to the side of the road a couple of times to let me throw up, but I didn't have to and we finally made it to the hospital.

There were no other patients in the waiting room, and we were taken to an examination room, where we waited for what seemed like forever. First there was a young female doctor. She gave me a quick examination, and said I'd probably had a concussion and I should take it very easy for at least five days, preferably a week. At that point I had no problems with not getting on a horse for a while.

Then she sent me to have X-rays. Because my knee was so badly swollen, she thought I might have broken something. We also had to wait forever for an X-ray.

My mother offered to get me something to drink, but I didn't want anything. My head hurt, I felt generally rotten and was freezing even though it was hot outside and the sun was shining. More than anything I wanted to close my eyes and go lie in a corner. But there were other people waiting, and I didn't dare lie down on a couch.

Finally our name was called, and they took X-rays of my knee. Then we had to wait over an hour for the results.

It was almost 5 p.m. when we finally could go home. The X-rays showed that there was nothing seriously wrong with my knee. It had only swollen up so badly because it had had such a heavy blow.

They gave me a pair of crutches and a whole lot of advice, mostly not to move too much and to take it easy.

I wasn't even supposed to think about riding a horse, and to tell the truth, I wasn't yearning to ride one anyway.

When we finally got home, I went straight to my room and crawled into bed. It was cool and pleasant in my room even though it was so hot outside. I fell asleep almost immediately and didn't wake up until 9 p.m.

When I awoke I felt a lot better already. Through the half-open window I could hear my father mowing the lawn, and smell that summery smell of freshly mown grass on a hot June evening.

I lay completely still and realized to my surprise that I didn't feel so bad at all. My headache was almost gone and my knee still hurt, but not so badly as before.

I decided to call Mike, and sat up in bed and grabbed my phone. I was, of course, very curious to know what was going on. But nothing happened when I pressed the numbers. The telephone was dead as a doorknob. Then I remembered that the batteries were dead, and I hadn't thought to recharge them.

Angry at myself, I grumbled and plugged the phone and charger in. Just then the door opened and my sister peered in. She actually looked normal, wearing a T-shirt and shorts, her hair in a pony tail and no makeup or green slime on her face, I thought as I stretched out.

"Were you sleeping?" she whispered, although she could see that I wasn't.

"No," I answered. "What is it?"

"Mike said to say hi," said Sophia. She came into the room and sat at the foot of the bed. "He just called a while ago."

"Oh, really," I answered casually, trying not to show how happy I was to hear it.

"Yep," she said, and let out that treacherous laugh I knew all too well.

"My God, he's cute!" Sophia gushed. "I know I wouldn't mind if he wanted to have a cup of coffee with me, or, who knows, maybe even invite me to the movies."

"Don't even think about it," I snarled and my sister screamed with laughter.

"Gotcha! You like him, don't you? Maybe you're even in love with him. You of all people, who never thought anything like that would happen to you because boys are all sooo stupid."

"Shut up," I mumbled, "It's bad enough you got me to admit it. What did he say?"

"We didn't talk very long," answered Sophia. "He said that."

Right then Mom came into my room with a cup of tea and some sandwiches on a tray, and Sophia stopped talking.

"And, how are you feeling now?" asked my mom solicitously and put the tray down on a little table next to my bed. "I heard you two talking and thought I'd bring you something to eat right away."

"Oh, thanks," I said hurriedly. "I'm as hungry as a wolf."

And I was too. I attacked those sandwiches and they were gone in a minute.

"I'm so glad you're feeling better," said my mother and smiled at me. "I'll go back downstairs, but you just yell if you want anything else."

109

"I can bring it to you," offered Sophia.

If Mom was surprised by Sophia's sudden attack of helpfulness, she didn't show it.

"OK, tell me," I said, as soon as mom was down the last step. "What did the old guy say when he came to get Fireflight?"

"Who was going to get him?" asked Sophia. "Fireflight's still with Hans and Maggie."

I stared at her in disbelief.

"What do you mean? The old guy was coming today to pick up Fireflight, wasn't he? At least that's what he said last night."

"That's what everybody thought, so this morning Mike and Hans went to Mike's friend's house to pick up Fireflight. They'd just gotten back with him, when the old guy phoned up to say he unfortunately had to go away for a few days, and he asked if Fireflight could stay at their place while he was gone."

"That's strange," I said, surprised. "This is the same guy who was so obsessed with picking up Fireflight that he turned up in the middle of the night wanting to take him."

"Well," Sophia continued, "Hans is so mad at the old guy for causing Mike all this trouble that he says if the thieves show up again they can just take Fireflight, it's fine with him! He doesn't care what happens, as long as they stay away from his property. And he's going to charge the old guy for all the damage those guys have done."

I couldn't suppress a laugh. I could just see Hans now, tearing his hair out because of Fireflight and everything that had happened. But when it occurred to me that he was probably wound up over Maverick's being in his stable, and the friendship between Mike and me, I stopped laughing.

"Do you know what else?" asked my dear sister as she giggled. "Dad is really mad at you, because you put Maverick in Hans and Maggie's stall last night."

I winced because I was feeling so guilty. That was really just like Dad, to find out about that. I had hoped to keep it a secret, but I guess that wasn't possible any more. I was afraid of my father's reaction, because he loved that old horse more than anything, and he surely was aware that things could have turned out really badly for Maverick.

"Dad was more upset that something might have happened to Maverick than about your little brush with death," Sophia continued. It was liked she'd read my mind.

I let out a deep sigh.

"But you don't have to worry. Mom told him he can't come up here and yell at you," said Sophia. "And she told him that you couldn't have known that they would take the wrong horse, and that Maverick didn't get hurt at all last night."

"Who told Mom and Dad everything?" I asked, and Sophia looked away, a little embarrassed.

"I told them most of it, then Maggie came and told them the rest."

I stretched back down in my bed and closed my eyes. I felt tired again.

"Do you want another sandwich?" she asked. I shook my head.

"No thanks, I'm just really tired."

"One more thing," she said in a half-whisper.

I looked at her.

"Mike said you could call him around 10 p.m. He'll be back then."

I looked at the clock, which said 9:57 p.m., and smiled at my sister.

"Thanks for the message. And close the door behind you."

Sophia grinned as she left my room. I tried Mike's number.

We talked for a long time. First about Fireflight and what had happened, and then about a lot of other things. I can't remember all the details any more, but one thing I'll never forget is the electric feeling I got having his voice so close to my ear…It sounded unimaginably wonderful!

The room was bathed in the dark blue of the summer sky and a warm breeze rustled the treetops. I felt very special, like I'd been changed into somebody else who didn't resemble little horse-crazy Sara Scaredycat any more. It felt kind of pleasant, but at the same time it was exciting.

When I said good night to Mike a lot later, I was in seventh heaven. I smiled into space, sank into my bed and closed my eyes. Somewhere in the room I heard a mosquito, but I didn't have the energy to turn on the light and kill it. If it wants to bite me, it'll bite me, I thought as I slipped blissfully into sleep.

The next morning I woke up around 10 a.m., but I lay in bed awhile before getting up, getting dressed, and going downstairs. My sister was already in the kitchen reading a magazine. Mom and Dad were nowhere around.

"There's hot water in the kettle if you want tea," said Sophia, without looking up from the fashion page of her magazine.

When I got a coffee mug from the cupboard, though, she looked at me in disbelief.

"You're drinking coffee? Are you feeling all right?"

"I'm fine," I answered as I poured some ground coffee into a filter. "I like coffee."

"Well, that's news," said Sophia and grinned meaningfully. "I'll bet I know who got you to like coffee."

"Shut up," I sniffed. I wasn't interested in talking about him with her if she was going to use that challenging, know-it-all tone of voice. I was afraid she was going to make fun of what I felt for Mike. Sometimes I wished my tiring little sister would just disappear down a hole!

I kept my mouth shut and poured myself some cereal and milk, put it on a tray with my coffee, and went outside to eat. I sat on a bench with an old horse magazine, leafing through it distractedly, slurping my coffee in between bites of cereal.

After breakfast I put on my bikini, and went to lie in the sun while I read. Then I looked through a couple of pages in my sister's magazine, and it occurred to me that maybe I should care more about my looks.

I'd actually never worn makeup, while my sister was an expert at it. And the question of fashion… If your favorite clothes are jeans and a sweatshirt, then the latest fashion isn't that important. But maybe I should find something fun to wear. Because, what if, say, Mike invited me out to the movies with him? It wouldn't do to turn up in my old torn jeans or T-shirt from the tractor dealer.

My cell phone was next to me, but it wasn't ringing. Finally I started to wonder if it was even working, but there was nothing wrong with it. There was nothing to do but wait for Mike to call.

But he didn't call, and time crawled on. We ate lunch, I lunged Fandango a little, and Dad wanted Sophia to practice for her contest, which was coming up soon. Mom complained that her roses were getting eaten up by bugs, I drank more coffee (to the astonishment of my whole family) and was beginning to really like it, and I even tidied up my room.

We ate dinner and watched a little TV. I played cards with my sister for a while, until we started fighting because (as usual) she was cheating. Then I went upstairs, to my room, and lay on my bed. That was it.

When I'd gotten into bed, I gazed longingly at my cell phone, and again I was almost convinced that it must be broken.

I turned the ringer off, slipped to the hallway and called my cell phone number with the house phone. I checked the number on the display and saw that everything was fine with my phone.

Why hadn't Mike called me? Had anything happened, and if so, what? Why hadn't I heard from him? I had at least a thousand theories why he hadn't called, each one more tragic than the previous. But they all came down to the same thing: he thought I was definitely a nice girl but still too young and immature, and it was better if we didn't see each other any more. The phone call last night was purely out of politeness, because I'd helped him despite all the trouble between the two families.

I cuddled up, depressed, with a horse book, but I'd only just started reading when Sophia practically sneaked into my room in her nightgown and slippers.

"Did he call yet?" she whispered inquisitively. I sighed.

"No, he hasn't."

"Then there must not have been any new developments," she said, and yawned.

"No, I guess not."

"Well, you seem in a bad mood," grumbled Sophia. "I thought you were so happy you two had met."

"He hasn't called again," I said somberly. "What if he doesn't call any more?"

Sophia smiled and gave me a reassuring pinch on the leg, as if she were the older and wiser of the two of us.

"Be patient," she urged me. "He'll call you soon, for sure. It's really clear he's interested in you. He just doesn't want to come on too strong."

115

"Do you think so?" I asked hopefully, and my sister nodded.

"Of course. The guy is just worried about people finding out about you two. You just need to wait a little."

"Maybe I should just call him," I said and looked at the clock. "Or is it too late?"

"Don't," said Sophia firmly. "Let him call you. Give him some time."

I nodded and felt terribly stupid. It's almost unthinkable that you have to ask your little sister for advice about how to deal with boys. That was pretty embarrassing!

"How's it going with Alexandra's big brother?" I asked, and Sophia looked confused for a second.

"Oh, you mean Matt? No, there's nothing between us. We're just good friends. I met another guy though. His name's Fred. He's really great and..."

My sister started on a long description of all Fred's fantastic qualities, and I listened absent-mindedly. When she was done I nodded and said, "Well, lots of luck with Robert."

"His name's Fred!" she hissed. "You're not listening to me – as usual!"

"Of course I was listening," I answered and looked up, "but you know I'm not good with names."

Sophia stuck her tongue out at me and left the room, and finally I had some peace.

I was tired and soon turned out the light. The phone call with Mike from last night came up in my thoughts again, and I had to laugh softly.

Sophia was right. He had to be the one to call. Maybe he would tomorrow.

But Monday and Tuesday passed and nothing happened. Mike didn't call, and I got sadder and sadder. What could have happened? What if Hans had forbidden him to speak to me or see me? Could Hans really do something like that? I wouldn't put it past him, I had to admit, because he and my father were still mad at each other, and if Hans was in a bad temper he could do anything. For Mike, keeping his job was probably more important than seeing me, I thought, humiliated.

What if he'd met another girl? I knew that Hans and Maggie had a very pretty daughter named Susie, who was 22 and knew all about horses. Maybe she'd come home from college and they'd fallen for each other and... I didn't want to think about it any more.

When I woke up on Wednesday morning, I decided that I'd waited long enough. I would never fall in love again, that was sure. Boyfriends were not for me. Sophia could have fun with her Fred, Robert, Matt or whatever his name was this time. I'd stick to horses from now on. I sat up in bed, stretched my arms wide and thought it wouldn't be a bad idea to go for a little ride with Fandango. My knee already felt a lot better. The swelling had gone down a lot, and I hadn't had any headache in the last couple of days.

I mustn't let my lack of a love life keep me from riding, I thought grumpily, and I pulled on an old yellow T-shirt with the logo of a weedkiller brand, and a pair of old cutoff jeans.

I took the pile of Sophia's magazines I'd more or less finished and threw them on Sophia's bed as I passed her room. The clothes stores and cosmetics departments

117

weren't going to get any of my money, because I wasn't planning on buying any new clothes or makeup, I thought bad-humoredly and went into the kitchen to make some breakfast.

I took my usual place outside, so I could eat in peace. My sister and Alexandra were in the kitchen cackling like a pair of excited geese. I couldn't stand being near the two of them.

The sun was shining in a fairy-tale blue sky, it smelled like fresh hay, and the bumblebees were humming in Mom's flowerbeds, but I didn't notice any of it. It all left me cold. For all I cared it could have been November.

The scene ended with me going back to my room and flopping on the bed. I had never felt so miserable before. Why wasn't he calling me any more? It would have been better if we'd never met, then I wouldn't be feeling this sad and...

Just then the telephone began to ring. At first I thought it was something else, but it kept ringing. I grabbed my cell phone and quickly piped "Hellooo." It occurred to me too late that I should have waited with the hello, to come over cooler and more in-different.

It was Mike! My heart started to beat faster, and I noticed how nervousness gave me a dry throat. Mike, on the other hand, was his usual self. He asked about my knee and wanted to know about every little thing.

Then he told me that Fireflight was still staying at Hans's stable. Mike was taking care of him and rode him every day. They hadn't heard anything from the old guy. He didn't answer messages they'd left on the answering machine, and neither of his two stable boys knew where

118

he was. It was all very strange and Hans was boiling with rage, said Mike. I could imagine that easily. Hans, of course, would have little interest in feeding and caring for somebody else's horse, he was such a miser.

I was just wondering if there was any particular reason Mike had called, when he came to the point.

"I have to drive to the racetrack to get some papers for somebody who's training one of Hans's horses. Do you feel like coming along?"

For a second, I was taken aback, but then I felt totally happy. Of course I felt like coming along.

Mike told me that Hans was out making hay. My parents weren't home either; my mom was at work and my dad was helping his brother with haymaking too.

That meant that no one would see if I drove away with Mike – that was what I thought, after I hung up. Beaming with happiness I stormed down to the kitchen where my sister was still jabbering with Alexandra.

"Quick," I said, "I want to borrow your top, the white ribbed one that looks so cute."

"Forget it," my sister answered resolutely. "You keep your hands off it."

"Oh, please," I begged. "Mike just called. I'm going with him to the racetrack to pick up some papers for a trainer that Hans knows."

"Well, what do you know," reacted Sophia, curious. "Do Hans and Maggie know you're going with him?"

I shook my head.

"No. And Mom and Dad don't either. And you two keep your mouths shut!"

The two looked at each other and burst out laughing.

119

Alexandra said, "Come on, give her the top. After all she got Mike to pick us up when we missed the bus that time. Don't be so mean, Sophia." At first Sophia looked like she objected, but eventually she nodded.

"OK, you can borrow it. But don't get it dirty. Take a shower and comb your hair before you leave. You look horrible!"

I made a grimace.

"Do you mean it? But of course I'll have a shower. But I've got to hurry, because he'll be here in 20 minutes!"

I disappeared into the bathroom to get pretty.

The drive to the racetrack took almost an hour. We took the freeway since there wasn't much traffic so early in the afternoon. Mike put a fantastic CD in the car's player, and we had the best time talking about all kinds of things. I felt fine and happy, and it was almost like the previous two horrible days hadn't happened.

When we got to the racetrack, Mike parked the car by the fence and we walked over the gatekeeper, who was sitting reading the paper and drinking a soda. At first he was hesitant about letting us in to the stables, but when Mike told him that we knew the trainer and had to pick up some papers from him, he let us in.

The trainer's stable was all the way in back of a row of stalls. Since I'd never been to a real racetrack before, I looked around inquisitively.

There were horses everywhere. Shining, strong-muscled magnificent thoroughbreds, moving with a dancer's grace over the tracks and paths. Here and there between the various stables were small sandy rings surrounded by white picket fences, and they were full of horses.

I saw several thoroughbreds I really wanted to take home with me. One was a cinnamon-colored mare who couldn't stand still for a second. When she ran it was like watching a whirlwind, and when she streamed past us with a short dark-blond boy on her back it was as if she were floating.

The racetrack was further back. I could hear the thunder of hoofbeats, and suddenly a group of horses passed me at a full gallop.

Mike had to laugh when he saw how interested I was in it all.

"We can walk around a little and look at everything if you feel like it," he said. "I know a few of the trainers. One is a really nice girl named Cathy."

"Wow," I said. "I'd love to. How exciting!"

"My father trained a few of the thoroughbreds here. That's how I got the job with Hans and Maggie. You know what they say, it's not *what* you know, it's *who* you know…"

I nodded. He'd already mentioned that that first morning, when we sat in his kitchen eating bread and jam. It was hard to believe that it was only a week ago. It seemed like ages!

We reached the first stable, and Mike said hello to a trainer. This one was short and skinny, had close-cropped hair and a rough beard and nonchalantly smoked a pipe which was hanging from a corner of his mouth. He looked grumpy when we walked into the tack room, where he kept the folder with the papers we'd come to get in a closet.

"Too bad we didn't sell that horse," he muttered to Mike. Mike nodded.

"Yeah, but there'll be other opportunities," answered

Mike. "Hans says she's done really well in practice the last little while."

The man just lifted his nose a little.

"I'm sure he's right," he said as he took the pipe, which had gone out, from his mouth. "If she doesn't get up to speed pretty soon, she'll only be fit for dog food. You tell him that. I'll do everything I can, but I'm not a wizard. If she doesn't want to jump, she won't jump, it's as simple as that."

Still lost in his thoughts, he nodded the last words even more emphatically, stuck the pipe back in his mouth, mumbled a gruff "See you later," and disappeared down a corridor.

Mike took the file under his arm, and once we were back outside I asked him what that last exchange was all about. He said that the bearded man had a horse of Hans's that he had to train. It should have been sold but at the last minute the sale didn't go through. In the folder was the sales contract, which hadn't been signed, and the registration papers.

We strolled leisurely past the stables and looked around everywhere. After a while we came to some stables with fewer stalls where Cathy worked.

Cathy didn't look any older than 18, but she must have been at least 25 if she had her own horses in training. She was short and elegant, with long blond hair in a braid.

She was busy saddling a handsome dark-brown stallion, who continually put his ears back and tried to bite her. He didn't look like he'd calm down, but Cathy just laughed and patted his neck. Once she had fastened the girth, he was meek as a lamb.

"Hey, it's Mike!" she cried when she saw us walking towards her. "Nice to see you!"

After Mike introduced me to her, Cathy and he started to talk about what had happened since they'd seen each other last. In the meantime I looked around some more.

The stall was a little bit neglected-looking, and it was ready for a new coat of paint, but the corridor was spanking clean and it smelled nice and fresh.

The seven horses stood peacefully eating in their stalls.

I was only half listening to what Cathy and Mike were telling each other, but suddenly my ears pricked up when I heard the name Fireflight.

"Yeah, he was here at the racetrack," said Cathy to Mike. "He's Lind's own horse, but he's not especially fast. Of course Lind would be happy if he'd won a few races, so he could sell him for more money."

"Has he won anything yet?" asked Mike with interest, and Cathy thought for a second.

"No idea," she answered. "He wasn't bad as a 2 year old, but since then he's had problems with his front legs. But why do you want to know? Your father has never had anything to do with Lind and his horses, has he?"

"No. I was just wondering," said Mike breezily. "We just passed his stable, and I got curious."

He shrugged his shoulders as if it didn't matter, and started talking about something different. I really would have liked to know why he hadn't told Cathy that Fireflight was in Hans and Maggie's stable, but I kept my mouth shut. Maybe he'll tell me later, I thought.

After a few minutes she took the bridle down and put the bit in the stallion's mouth. She asked if we wanted to see how fast she could go around the track, which of course we did.

There were still a few horses on the track, and I longingly stared out over the wide expanse. You could really get up to speed here, I thought dreamily and stared at a few chestnut horses as they galloped past us.

"Would you ever like to ride a thoroughbred?" Mike asked, as if he'd read my mind.

"Oh, yes," I said with a deep sigh. "That would be amazing!"

Mike burst out laughing.

"It's one of the best experiences you can ever have," he said. "It's like nothing else on earth. The whole track is empty in front of you, and the horse feels like an arrow shot from a bow over the track. It's just fantastic!"

He went silent and together we watched as Cathy and her horse warmed up at the edge of the track.

The dark-brown stallion jumped and danced around so wildly I couldn't imagine Cathy being able to stay on his back. But it looked like she'd become one with the horse and it seemed to me she was even laughing at how rambunctious he was.

After a little while they went into a canter and in a flash this nervous animal was transformed into a professional racehorse. In an instant the stallion had gone from bucking around to a completely different tempo while maintaining his full concentration.

His legs moved as fast as drumsticks playing a drum roll and he took each jump with his back legs well forward under his body, while Cathy was bent deep over his neck, completely relaxed.

It all looked so simple, but when they rode past us we could see the stallion bathed in sweat, and Cathy's face red from exertion.

"Wow," she said later, out of breath, "this horse forces you to do your best when you ride him."

"He's beautiful," I said, stressing the words because I really meant it.

"I agree with you completely," Cathy answered with a laugh. "He was the best 2 year old on this track last year, and he's won the most often. He's won almost all his races this year too. He's really wonderful!"

She stroked his neck, and Mike smiled at her.

"He's amazing," he said. "You should have a horse like this in your own stable."

"I think so too," Cathy nodded. "I went through a couple of hard years when I started working as a trainer. But now I feel like it's starting to pay off. I wouldn't do it like the owner of Fireflight did. You know, that guy we were talking about earlier."

"Oh no?" asked Mike. "What do you mean?"

We had come to the stable door and Cathy had dismounted. She stopped talking and just gave us a nod as a sign that we should follow her into the stable.

Mike and I hurried in after her and once we were inside, Mike closed the door behind us.

Cathy took the small, polished racing saddle off the stallion and hung it over the wall of the stall before continuing in a low voice:

"I just overheard a couple of guys saying that this Lind guy is going to go bankrupt sooner or later. Supposedly he owes lots of money to the feed dealer who always sells me his expensive hay. But it might be only a rumor, I can't say for sure. I haven't seen him for a whole day. Somebody said he might have left the state."

"Bankrupt?" said Mike, astonished. "But he always has a full stable and lots of horses to train."

Cathy nodded.

"It's often that way. Also, he's not so young anymore, and he's not every popular either. He always gets into arguments with everybody, and he drinks a lot too. That probably has a lot to do with it too."

"You can't get too deep into debt, or people will bring their horses to train somewhere else," said Mike, and Cathy added, "My neighbor just bought one of Lind's horses last week. And that was a good horse, not a one you'd just sell off like that!"

Mike nodded. Cathy led her horse to a washing area and started washing him off with lukewarm water. I hoped she'd tell us more about Fireflight's owner, but she didn't say another word about him.

Instead she started talking with Mike about his father's horses, and eventually it was time to get back home.

When we stepped out of the stable into the brilliant sunshine, Mike said he'd gotten very hungry. He suggested getting lunch somewhere.

"Couldn't we eat something here?" I asked, because I'd seen that there was a cafeteria here.

"Are you crazy!" said Mike with a grin. "They make the food here out of the horses that didn't race fast enough."

We both had to laugh. We walked to the car, got in and

drove a little further to a side street where Mike knew there was a nice pizza place. You could even sit outside and eat.

We ordered a large pizza and while we waited for it, we talked under a big parasol.

Sitting outside with him was wonderful, and I was enjoying every second. The pizza was delicious. I couldn't finish my half, but Mike took care of his half and the rest of mine.

Afterwards we had some coffee and I had to admit I felt really grown up, sitting like that in a restaurant, eating, ordering coffee, and talking with Mike. This was definitely the best day of my life. It couldn't get much better than this.

Later we strolled lazily back to the car which was parked a little farther up the street. We had to cross a busy intersection to get to it, and we waited for a long time, thinking the light would never turn green.

While we were standing there, I saw a familiar car approaching from the distance – the old guy's blue pickup!

"Mike! See that car?" I asked excitedly and pulled on his sleeve.

Mike followed my gaze, and let out a long, low whistle.

"Can you see who's driving?" he asked as we stared at it.

"No, the sun's in my eyes. Can you recognize anybody?"

"I thought so," answered Mike and looked at the truck as it headed for the freeway entrance. "It was Lind, Fireflight's owner!"

On the way back, we exchanged our thoughts about what we'd seen and done today. Why had Lind not come by or called at Hans's place? Was it true he was almost bankrupt? And why was he driving around in town, while Cathy had said that he was out of the state?

Something wasn't right, that was all we could say. We had a lot of new information but it only brought up new questions. When we drove over the gravel road to my house, it was already 3:30 p.m. There was a car behind us and when I turned around, I saw that it was our family's car.

"Oh no," I groaned. "My father is coming home. This is bad!"

Mike looked in the rear view mirror and sighed.

"Will he be mad if he sees you with me in the car?"

"He sure will," I answered, "but I don't care. I'll go out with whoever I want to."

Mike gave me a sidelong glance and stopped right before our driveway, while Dad drove past us and stopped the car in front of our house. He studied Mike's car, and I knew he'd seen me.

"Thanks for taking me along," I said and smiled at Mike. "I had a really great day."

"So did I," he said and returned my smile.

Our eyes met, and suddenly it was embarrassingly quiet in the car. I felt really awkward and didn't know what to say next. Mike had the next word.

"I think you probably ought to get out now. Your father's coming over."

I turned around and saw my father walking swiftly over to Mike's car, and thought I'd better take his advice.

"See you later!" Mike said, and shut the car door behind me.

The he disappeared in a cloud of dust as he went towards Hans and Maggie's place, and I walked to meet my father, who was looking especially angry.

"Where have you been?" he asked indignantly, when we'd met halfway.

"I was in town with Mike," I answered and gave him an exaggerated smile. "Why?"

Dad glared after Mike's car as it disappeared.

"I don't like you seeing that boy," he said. "I'm sure he'll be getting you to do stupid things."

"Oh, come on, Dad. He's really sweet and nice."

"He was nice until he got my … my Maverick into Hans's stall. Just imagine if anything had happened to him!"

I looked at my father. Now it was becoming clear why my dad was in such a bad mood – he still hadn't forgiven Mike and me for that.

"I know that made you mad, but that wasn't our fault,"

I said trying to calm him down as we walked to the house. "If Sophia hadn't…"

Suddenly I remembered that Mom and Dad still had no clue that Sophia and Alexandra had gone to town without their permission, and I tried to think of something to turn the conversation around.

"If Sophia hadn't what?" asked my father suspiciously. I sighed.

"If Sophia had come home right away and had opened the door for me, it wouldn't have happened," I continued, and thought that at least it was partly true. My father mumbled something I couldn't make out and went into the house ahead of me. My mother was busy in the kitchen unloading groceries from a few bags, and seemed in a good humor. I was hoping that Dad was through with our conversation, but luck was not on my side.

"Sara went out with that Michael guy or whatever his name is and they've been driving around. Do you approve of this?"

"But honey," answered my mother surprised, "I think Sara's old enough to choose her friends, don't you?"

"I just don't like this friendship," he responded angrily and looked sidelong at me. "Who knows what he'll get up to after this."

Mom smiled at him lovingly.

"It won't be that bad, you'll see. Maggie said that he's a nice and sensible young man. It'll be fine to let Sara be friends with him."

I gave my mother a grateful look, and she gave me a wink. It was nice that at least one person in our family besides me could see that Mike was a great person.

The rest of the afternoon went slowly. I was tired and had a nagging pain in my knee. I shouldn't have left my crutches at home, I thought, lying on my bed leafing through old horse magazines. But now it was too late to complain.

Shortly after seven I heard my cell phone's merry melody. It was Mike.

"I told Hans that we saw Fireflight's owner today, and since then he's been trying to reach him on the phone or get in touch through somebody else. But everyone he talks to says he's out of the state. Do you think we made a mistake?"

"I don't know," I answered uncertainly. "I have to admit my memory of that night's a little shaky – it was pretty dark out and I did have a concussion. But the car we saw today was his, I'm absolutely sure of it."

"Maybe he drove another car out of state and lent this one to a friend," said Mike and even I could see that was possible.

"What would you say to a cup of coffee?" Mike suggested and I laughed and answered, "Great!" But then I thought of something.

"Won't Hans be mad if I show up at his house?"

"Hans and Maggie are out tonight," said Mike. "They won't be back before midnight."

I thought for a minute. If my dad heard that I wanted to go over to Hans and Maggie's, he'd protest violently. In any case it would surely start an argument. But my mom seemed to like Mike. I decided to ask her, because she would say yes, and then Dad couldn't complain that I hadn't asked permission.

Happy to have solved that problem, I told Mike I'd come by later that evening. After a quick shower, I went downstairs and out into the garden, where my mother was kneeling at a flower bed.

"Look, the seeds have sprouted," she called, beaming with pleasure, and pointed at a few tender green shoots.

"Wow, great," I said, even though I didn't have any idea what kind of seeds she was talking about. "I was going to go over to Mike's for a little while. Is that OK?"

My mother looked at me and smiled.

"Of course."

"Where's Dad?" I asked and my mother looked over at our driveway.

"I think he went over to George and Mia's. They're making hay and as usual the tractor was causing some trouble."

I knew that something was usually wrong with George's tractor, so that meant that Dad was going to be there for a while. In good spirits, I picked up my crutches and hobbled over to the road to our neighbors' place. It was a gorgeous warm summer evening, and I was enjoying every minute of it. How wonderful life could be!

Mike's place already smelled like fresh coffee. I went to sit at the kitchen table and set my crutches against the chair.

Mike offered me an old horse magazine that he'd opened to an article about horse racing. At first I didn't understand what he wanted me to look at, but then he pointed at a black-and-white photo of a rider with a victory wreath. Next to him was a guy with bow legs, and according to the caption under the picture, that was Lind.

133

Unfortunately the picture was a little fuzzy, so I could just vaguely make out his face.

"He was going pretty fast when he passed us today," I said, "but you bet, that was the guy at the wheel."

"Well done," Mike agreed, "I think so too."

Suddenly something occurred to me that I'd thought about several times before but kept forgetting.

"Why did the old guy replace the car and trailer? Do you have any idea why he'd do that?" I asked.

"Replaced?" asked Mike. "What do you mean?"

"You told me that when he brought Fireflight here he came in some old beat-up car. But the pickup and trailer looked pretty new and in really good shape. So he replaced the car."

Mike was silent for a long time.

"Maybe his car was having trouble," he said at last. "Remember, you saw him in that parking lot looking at the engine."

I nodded.

"I'd forgotten about that. Is Fireflight still here?" I asked. Mike nodded.

"You bet, he's in his stall. We can go over and say hi to him later if you like."

"Sure, I'd like to," I said. "Is he doing all right?"

"He's fine," Mike confirmed, "but he's really much too slow. He'll never be a good race horse."

"Too bad." And I meant it, because I liked Fireflight a lot.

We drank our coffee and again, the time flew by. We talked about all sorts of things, and I noticed that we had a whole lot in common with each other.

Then it was almost 11 p.m., and I knew it was time to get on my crutches and go home, even though I really didn't want to. I would rather have sat up all night at the kitchen table talking with Mike.

The yard in front of Mike's little house was quiet. The soft summer breeze caressed my face and in a word, everything was idyllic. Mike offered to walk part of the way with me, but first we went to the stable to look in on Fireflight.

We had just come to the stable door when we heard a strange noise from the back of the stable. It was sort of a hissing noise and there was also light coming from inside. I couldn't really describe it any other way.

"I'll just go back and see what's going on," said Mike with a nervous little laugh.

He walked away while I opened up the stable door and hobbled in on my crutches. Oddly enough, the light wouldn't go on, but I didn't worry about it, and walked over towards Fireflight's stall.

The stallion was restless, even though it was practically the middle of the night. He was stamping back and forth in his stall, and now and then would neigh loudly and shrilly. He was obviously irritated about something, and was shaking his beautiful head around and kicking against the sides of the stall so that the whole stable was shaking.

I tried to calm him down by talking softly, then I became aware of a strange smell. I sniffed and tried to figure out what it could be, but although it smelled familiar I couldn't put my finger on it...

I looked around the half-dark stable and discovered

135

there was a big pool of some liquid on the cement floor, right next to the door to the manure pile.

Suddenly I knew what it was – that smell was gasoline! But why would somebody spill gas on the floor of a stable? In the same instant I knew there was just one answer. And my hunch was confirmed a second later when I smelled smoke.

I shivered when I realized what danger Fireflight was in. Now I heard Mike screaming outside too, and everything started to crackle and snap, and for a second I didn't know what to do.

There was only one thing to do: I had to get Fireflight out of there as fast as I could!

When I look back on it now, it seemed like everything happened in slow motion. I knew that I probably didn't have more than a couple of seconds and not more than a couple of minutes.

I took Fireflight's halter from its hook and undid the door of the stall, before putting it on. But it was impossible to get anywhere near the stallion, who was very frightened right now. He was flailing about so much he almost fell into his straw.

It was obvious that he'd trample me if I went inside his stall, so I stood in front of him with his halter in my hand. I tried to calm him down by talking to him, although I felt pretty panicky myself and my throat was so dry I could only get out a scratchy noise.

Maybe Fireflight understood me after all, or maybe not, but suddenly he stood still, staring at me with big fearful eyes. His nostrils were flared; of course he could smell the biting smoke more intensely than I could. When he neighed, it sounded like he was calling for help.

He reared up on his hind legs and went up so high that I was afraid he would fall over backwards, and I could only stand there and watch. At the same time I knew that the chances of getting him out of there in one piece were getting smaller by the second. More and more gray smoke was filling the stable, and it wouldn't be long before I would be forced to escape to the outside without Fireflight just to save myself.

In some miraculous way, Fireflight must have understood that I was trying to help him. When he was back on all four legs, he took a couple of steps towards me and stuck his head in my direction.

In a fraction of a second I was able to get the halter on him. He willingly followed me towards the door.

The smoke was getting thicker and thicker, and I almost couldn't breathe. It was now almost completely dark in the stable. My eyes were running with tears, my throat was burning and I tried to hold an arm in front of my face to protect myself, while I pulled Fireflight along towards the stable's big front door.

Behind me, I could hear the stable walls hissing, spattering, and cracking. The door to the manure pile was probably already on fire, I figured while desperately trying not to let go of Fireflight's halter. He'd started to buck and rear up again. One moment I would be standing with both feet firmly on the ground, and the next I was hanging in the air on the halter, with him shaking his head back and forth to get loose.

At the moment we reached the door, we heard a terrible crash behind us as the window in the door to the manure pile was blown out of its frame by the force. The flames quickly spread to the inside of the stable, but with a last desperate try I got the door open and pulled Fireflight towards me.

"Outside, now!" I screamed, and Fireflight forced his way through the door opening with me hanging on his halter.

Although he was dancing around wildly, I managed to get the door closed, and we ran along the path to the paddock.

Fireflight knew where we were, and before we'd reached the paddock had torn himself loose and trotted through the open gate. I closed it behind him and turned around, numbed with shock and my whole body trembling.

The stable was burning like a straw house, with tall yellow flames that looked like they reached to the sky. The building must have been completely soaked with gas, because it only took a couple of minutes for the whole place to be ablaze.

I had never seen anything like this in my life! The heat was incredible, and I took a couple of steps back to be further away from the awful sight. I realized that I still could have been trapped in there. It was only by pure luck that Fireflight had been able to escape.

At the same time I had a terrible thought and felt my stomach churning. Where was Mike? I'd heard his voice from in front of the stable not so long ago. I didn't want to think about it, but what if he'd gone into the stable to help me get Fireflight free! If only he hadn't...

"Mike!" I screamed as loudly as I could. "Where are you?"

I was doing my best, but with my hoarse voice I couldn't get much louder than the roar of the flames and the tremendous heat forced me back towards the fence, in back of which Fireflight was racing back and forth, crazed with fear.

I knew that I should call the fire department and go looking for Mike, but it was as if I couldn't control my body anymore. I couldn't move. I couldn't even cry. I just stood there, pressed against the fence, stiff from shock.

Then I saw someone coming towards me: it was Mike!

"There you are," he roared to raise his voice above the noise of the fire. "I was so worried about you! I thought that you were still in there! Oh, sweetie ..."

Mike threw his arms around my neck, and I hugged him hard and pressed my head against his shoulder. Then suddenly I was sobbing desperately. It was like a dam had broken. I didn't even notice my father and mother drive up or hear the squeal of tires as they stopped the car on the gravel driveway.

"What's happened?" shouted my father and ran over to us.

"The firemen are on their way," panted my mother. "Are there still any horses inside?"

Mike shook his head.

"There was only one horse in there and that was Fireflight. Sara managed to get Fireflight outside when the stable started to burn."

"Have you gone crazy!" my father shouted. He must have thought that I went into the stall after it started to burn. "What if you'd been trapped in there, just for the sake of that damn horse!"

"It wasn't on... there wasn't any fire at first," I said between sobs. "It only started after I was inside."

"Shut your mouth for once," my mother said indignantly to my father. "Can't you see she's in shock? She's alive, and that's the most important thing."

"Of course, I'm sorry, honey," answered Dad soothingly and stroked my hair tenderly, just like he used to do when I was little and was sad about something.

Afterwards I understood that he'd reacted so angrily because he was so upset.

A little later we could hear the sirens of the fire engines. I didn't know who had called them, but I found out later it was my father. He had seen the flames and smoke while he was on his way home and had called them right away on his cell phone. At that point he didn't know I was there too.

"Now it's time to go home," my mother said resolutely to Mike and me. "We'll only be in the way here."

"I'm staying here," said Mike, who still had his arm around my shoulder.

"Me too," I said, although I felt more like going home, crawling in my bed and pulling up the covers over my head and having a good hard cry.

But standing there with Mike I felt so safe. My mother just let out a sigh.

"OK, then I'll stay here too, but we'll have to move aside so we're not in the way when the fire trucks get here. What a good thing Sophia's at Alexandra's."

I'll bet Sophia would see it differently, I thought and despite my condition I couldn't help smiling. Sophia would have given anything to be here now.

In the meantime the lights of the fire engines had reached our farm and the siren got louder and louder.

141

My mother and I walked slowly over to the house, while Mike and my father talked to the fire chief once he'd gotten out of the fire truck.

Mom put an arm around me, and we stood like that, watching Hans and Maggie's beautiful old stable become a smoking wet pile of ashes, charred beams and twisted iron struts.

The whole night was one long chaos and when I think back, I can't put all the events precisely in order. The police came, Hans and Maggie finally showed up and at last all of us were at our house in the kitchen, drinking coffee, at 4:30 a.m.

The stable was still burning in a few places, and the firemen thought it would take at least a couple of hours before the last ones would be under control. There was a weird stink hanging in the air and both farms were veiled in smoke, as the sun came up and announced an especially hot day.

The police wanted to question Mike and me right away, and we told them all we knew, but that really wasn't much. Neither one of us had noticed anything unusual, at least not until we'd gone to the stable to see Fireflight and heard that odd hissing. That was of course from the flames that had just caught, as they were just starting to spread, said Mike, and I thought so too.

Whoever had started the fire had set it in the circuit box at the back of the stable, so that it would look like it had been caused by a short circuit.

Mike also said that he'd seen somebody walking away

towards the woods. He thought it was someone short and moving slowly, but he couldn't be completely sure. He was shocked from the fire and panicked because he knew that Fireflight and I were in the stable, but felt nailed to the ground, and couldn't run inside.

For a while Mike had been convinced that I'd been killed in the fire with Fireflight.

After he was done, I made my statement. Mike sat next to me the whole time on the kitchen bench holding my hand. I felt safe and secure having him.

I hadn't noticed anything unusual either, until I'd gone into the stable and smelled gasoline. Bit by bit I told my story to the police officer, who made a few notes. As I finished I mentioned Sophia's suspicion that Fireflight's owner might have been trying to get rid of the horse. Hans, my father and the officer looked at me curiously.

"But Kalle Lind has no reason at all to get rid of that horse," said Hans firmly. "Fireflight is worth a lot more alive than dead, I can tell you that. And anyway, Lind is in Wisconsin now buying more horses."

Hans told the police officer that he'd been trying to reach Fireflight's owner all day but unsuccessfully. At last one of Lind's employees at the racetrack stables had told Hans that he apparently had gone away. That seemed to convince the officer that Lind was innocent, since he couldn't have come here and set the stable on fire last night if he was so far away.

"Kids," said the police officer to my parents as he closed his notebook, "they see mysteries everywhere. I was just the same when I was young. It's why I became a cop."

He gave me a kind little wink. I slumped in my chair and stared back, thinking he'd better take us seriously.

"But you could at least try to find Fireflight's owner and talk with him, can't you?" asked Mike. "This is serious! It's arson, and someone could have died as well. What if Sara was burned up alive in there!"

"Of course this is serious," answered the officer kindly, "but we can't get ahead of the investigation. We have to take it step by step, and we can't go around accusing people of something as serious as arson and attempted murder. Of course we want to speak with Fireflight's owner. I promise you we will."

Mike and I looked at each other, and then Mike said, "Sara and I were at the racetrack yesterday. We heard from one of the other trainers that Fireflight's owner is almost bankrupt."

"We're also sure he drove past us while we were waiting to cross the street," I said urgently. "He was driving the same blue pickup I saw him in on the forest road the other morning, and again when he came to get Fireflight in the middle of the night."

"Can't you see it all fits together?" Mike was really worked up. "He was trying to get Fireflight out of the way. He just wants everybody to think he's out of town."

"How can you be so sure it was the same car?" asked Hans cautiously. "Everybody I talked to yesterday said the same thing – Kalle's out of town. I'm sure there are witnesses to confirm that. And there are a lot of cars out there that look just like his."

"I'll never forget that car," I burst out, and stared right at Hans. "Not after he and his friend tried to get

Maverick in that trailer and take him away."

I was getting tired of all his putting me down, although I could understand he was in a bad mood. After all, his beautiful stable had just been burned to the ground and it must have been a huge shock for him.

"I'm just as convinced," Mike piped up. "Does anyone know how much Fireflight is insured for?"

Now the policeman started to look interested. He opened his notebook again and picked up the pen he'd laid on the kitchen table.

"Why didn't you say that earlier?" he asked.

Mike and I just looked at each other.

"We tried to, but you wouldn't believe us," I said and felt Mike squeeze my hand.

"Maybe now you understand that we're not just a couple of crazy kids making things up."

Then we had to go through the whole story another time, down to the tiniest details, and the officer wanted to talk over all the things that didn't make sense. I thought he'd never get enough of it, but eventually he did and left, and at some point everyone left and I was able to crawl into my nice soft bed. Outside, the warm sun was shining in a cloudless blue sky, but I didn't care. I just wanted to sleep! I fell asleep with the smell of smoke in my nose and even with my watery eyes. I was in a deep and dreamless sleep, until I was shaken rudely awake by someone shouting in my ear:

"Sara, wake up! You have to tell me everything! Come on, stupid sleepyhead! Wake up!"

146

In drama, the heroine is usually around for the exciting conclusion, but not in this one. By the time I was roused from my sleep by my sister, everything had been straightened out. I just didn't know it yet.

It was 3 p.m., and my sister was sitting at the foot of my bed, bursting with curiosity and pressing me to tell her everything that had happened. You could see how jealous she was of me, and despite everything I involuntarily laughed a little. This time it wasn't she who was at the center of the action, but me! Ha ha!

After I'd told her everything, I pointed out that for me it hadn't exactly been endless fun.

I tried to make her understand what it felt like to be so scared you couldn't move, even though you wanted to. While I was telling her I experienced the same helpless feeling of fear that overwhelmed me when I was in the stable staring at the flames, convinced that Mike was in there somewhere too, and I might die.

When my sister finally went away, I stretched out luxuriously in my bed. I was planning to get up at some point, but there really was no hurry. My knee hurt a lot, after all my activity last night and I suddenly realized that I'd tossed my crutches to the side in front of Fireflight's stall. I assumed there wasn't anything left of them by now but two piles of melted plastic with a piece of metal inside them.

Just as I felt like I was falling asleep again, I heard someone stomping up the stairs, and Sophia stormed into my room without knocking or anything. She was so excited she could hardly get a word out.

"Hurry up," she panted. "Maggie, Hans and Mike are all downstairs in the kitchen and they have a lot to tell you. Come on!"

In a flash she was gone, and I slowly got myself presentable and ready to do as she said. I wanted to hurry, but I just couldn't move very fast.

Feeling stiff as a board, I pulled on a sweater and jeans. I tied my hair out of my face with an elastic and saw in the mirror how bloodshot my eyes were, but I didn't care. I hobbled downstairs to the kitchen.

Mom, Dad, Hans, Maggie, and Mike were sitting around the kitchen table. Mom had just set cups and a pot of coffee on the table and was putting some pastries in the microwave.

Having Hans and Maggie at our table was a very unusual sight. It had been at least a year since they'd been to our house. But when I looked into Mike's blue eyes, I forgot everything else. Oh, how happy I was to see him.

"And now tell us!" my sister demanded to our visitors and sat down on a chair. "What happened?"

"The police arrested Fireflight's owner, and he's confessed to everything," said Hans calmly. "It's as simple as that."

"But what did he say?" asked my sister. "Was I right?"

"Yes, was she?" I wanted to know too.

Maggie had to laugh at our enthusiasm and Hans continued: "The old guy, as we'll call him, had had money troubles for a while. He'd hoped that Fireflight would earn him enough in prize money to keep up his training stables, but Fireflight isn't especially fast. He wins a race once in a while, but he's not a champion."

"But he should be," argued my father. "He has a good pedigree. He must have gotten good racing qualities. You would expect him to anyway."

"Of course," answered Hans, "but he just doesn't have it. Anyway, last winter the old guy raised the amount of money Fireflight's insured for, by a lot. That's probably when he came up with his plan. This season was pretty good for Fireflight and he did win some money, so he forgot about the plan, until recently..."

"And by 'the plan' you mean the plan to have Fireflight disappear and claim the insurance money," I said.

Hans nodded.

"Precisely. Fireflight was getting slower and slower in his last few races, and so finally Kalle Lind decided it was time to get him out of the way."

Hans took a sip of coffee before going on. "A few months ago he made all sorts of things happen that all pointed to one thing: that someone was after his horse."

"Who?" asked Sophia and I at the same time.

"He told anybody at the racetrack who would listen to

149

him that he'd been getting strange phone calls from people threatening to kill Fireflight. He also showed the police two threatening letters, and they took them seriously at the time," explained Maggie.

"And we all believed his lies," admitted Hans. "That Lind was famous for his bad temper. He got into arguments with everyone and owes a lot of people money. It wasn't that unlikely that something might happen to his horse one way or another."

"But it was all a tactic to make it look like someone else was responsible for the horse disappearing," Maggie filled in.

"But why did he want to steal Fireflight from you of all people?" I asked Hans. "Did he have a bone to pick with you two or something?" Hans shrugged his shoulders.

"Just the opposite. We'd never had much to do with each other, even though we knew each other. But a couple of weeks ago I ran into him at the racetrack in line at the cafeteria. I mentioned that we were going to England for a week and wanted to look up someone we both knew. Maybe that gave him the idea to stable Fireflight with us, so he could have him dis-appear from there."

"He told Hans that someone was after Fireflight so he wanted to stable him someplace safe for a while," Maggie went on. "That's how Hans put it when he came home, and it didn't surprise me at all, since the guy has such a hot temper and probably has made a lot of enemies."

It got very quiet in the kitchen. I thought over what Hans and Maggie had said, and it was clear to me it must have happened that way. I was sitting next to Mike on our kitchen bench and felt him putting his hand on top of mine.

My mother poured another round of coffee and passed the tray of pastries around. No one knew what to say any more. I did notice that Hans and my father had been avoiding looking at each other the whole time.

I realized this couldn't be easy for either of them.

Finally Sophia asked, "So what's going to happen now? What'll happen to Fireflight?"

"He can stay with us for a little while, and then we'll just have to see," Hans said carefully. "To be honest, I've thought about buying him. If the old guy does go bankrupt, Fireflight will cost a fraction of what he's worth. He's got good lineage, and he'd be good for breeding."

"A thoroughbred who's never won any important races doesn't have a chance as a sire," said my father like he was lecturing. "You ought to know that, Hans. You'd be better off with another stallion."

"Listen to him," sneered Hans.

"What do you know about breeding thoroughbreds? You've only got three geldings and not one thoroughbred. Might I point out that I grew up with thoroughbreds?"

"Enough!" interrupted my mother, and Hans and my father looked a little embarrassed. "Maggie and I are sick and tired of this constant bickering. You two are acting like a couple of 2 year olds."

"That's right," said Maggie, who was just as mad as my mother. "It's time to stop this nonsense once and for all. Why can't you behave like grown men from now on, so we can all just act like normal people with each other?"

151

"But…" started Dad and Hans at the same time, but they didn't get very far because the telephone rang. Sophia jumped up and ran to the hall to get it. Then she stuck her head in the doorway and smiled mysteriously.

"That was Alexandra. I'm going over there for a little while. Bye!"

"Sophia, wait! You've got a contest coming up and you and Camigo still have to…!" Dad called after her, but Sophia was already gone, and I heard the door close with a slam that shook the windows.

My father heaved a deep sigh.

"That darn girl! Now it'll be me who gets that stupid pony ready for tomorrow."

"I don't think you need to do that," I said calmly.

"But she's got a contest tomorrow," answered my dad and he looked at me as if I didn't understand. "Camigo still has to be washed, and his mane needs to be braided and…"

"I mean you should probably take her name off the list for tomorrow," I said quietly. "She's not really all that crazy about riding contests."

"Exactly," my mother agreed. "I think Sara's right. They don't both have to be champion riders."

She took my father's hand firmly in hers. Dad sat there without saying a word and looked terribly unhappy. I could see that it must be a heavy blow for him that Sophia didn't like horses as much as I did, but that was just the way it was.

Everybody's different, and Sophia just didn't like being with horses that much. That was a shame, because she was actually a good rider, but you can't force someone to do something they don't like. I had to admit I'd learned a lot in the last little while from my little sister. To begin with, I had to admit that we were totally different from each other, and it didn't matter. She was the way she was, and that was fine. Most important was that I loved her – just the way she was!

"Looks like we need another round of coffee now," said my mother and stood up. "Or maybe we should all have a drink?"

"I think it's about time to celebrate," answered Maggie. "And then you have to tell me how you got the bugs out of your roses. I think I have the same thing."

While the grown-ups kept up their conversation, Mike and I went outside and walked over to the paddock. Maverick and Camigo stood there looking very relaxed, and switching the flies off each other with their tails. When Fandango saw us he came right over to us.

He bumped his soft nose against me, as if he wanted to know why I hadn't been out to see him all day.

I scratched him behind his ear, which I knew he loved, and swatted away a couple of obstinate flies from around his head.

"Be patient until my knee gets better," I said to my dear sweet pony. "Then we'll go galloping through the woods again, I promise. And we'll make that jump we didn't get to last time."

Fandango whinnied and bumped his head against me so hard that I almost fell over. I scratched him a little longer and then he turned and walked away to find some fresh grass. I watched him go and burst out laughing.

He was just great, my pony, and we had a long summer ahead of us. We could still spend a lot of time together, practicing and galloping, before it got dark and cold.

Mike and I were still standing, hand in hand. I gazed at him. Our eyes met and he put his arms around me and held me tight.

I closed my eyes and felt the rough texture of his shirt against my chin. And we stayed that way for a long, long time, until he kissed me.

And at that moment I knew I was the happiest horse-crazy girl in the whole wide world.